YOUNG, RICH & BLACK

AN 'AFTERWARDS' NOVELLA

NIA FORRESTER

STILETTO PRESS

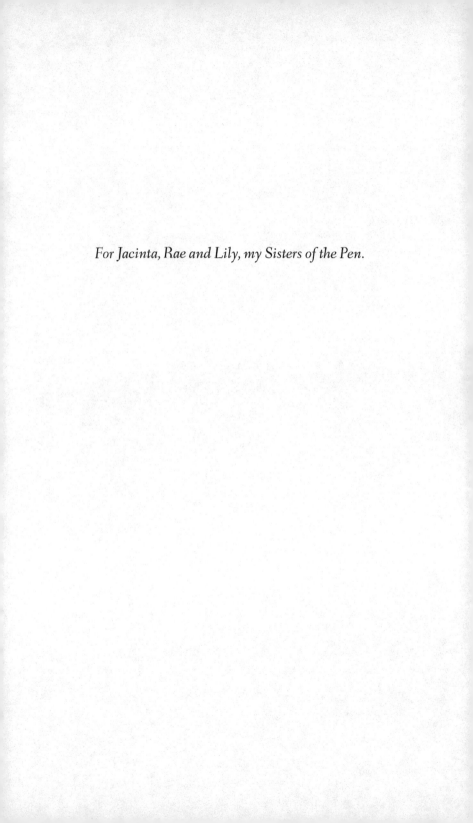

For Jacinta, Rae and Lily, my Sisters of the Pen.

FOREWORD

*This novella came into being when readers responded with such unexpected positivity to a 2016 holiday short story I wrote about the son of one of the main characters in my books **Afterwards** and **Afterburn**. I loved writing those books in part because Chris and Robyn, the main characters had such a rich and varied circle of friends and family. One of those family members was Deuce, who was featured in the holiday short and here, again, in this novella. He intrigued me because he is, as the title says, young, rich and Black — part of a rarefied life that was not earned through sports, a performing career, or longtime family wealth. He is the child of the Black nouveau riche, a generation we're only just beginning to see come into new adulthood.*

I wonder sometimes about how these young people going to fare in a world where there are still relatively few like them, and even fewer who understand them. How do they feel about the things that preoccupy lots of middle-class young people of color: race, identity politics, interracial relationships, and the relationship of all those things to social justice? I wanted to explore those questions through Deuce. And also, of course, give you a little sweetness, in the form of a good, not-so-old-fashioned love story.

Happy Reading,
    Nia

ONE

"Dude. Are you serious with this?"

"Sir, I asked you to step out of the car."

"Yeah, but why?"

"Are you refusing to comply?"

"Nah, officer, he's not refusing to comply. Deuce, get out the damn car."

Glancing over at Kaleem, in the passenger seat, Deuce sighed and disengaged the seatbelt, unlocking, then opening the door of his brand spanking new Range Rover, and stepping out onto the blacktop. It was cold outside, bitterly so, which only made him resent the command even more. He sized up the police officer standing in front of him—maybe late twenties, reddish-blonde hair and ruddy complexion, icy-blue eyes, thin-lipped and grim-faced.

"License and registration, please."

"For that I needed to get out of the car?"

"License and registration." The voice was a little louder now, the tone a little less friendly.

"Did I offend you, officer?" he asked.

When he got no answer, Deuce turned toward his vehicle once again and hesitated, looking back before reaching for the door handle. "Can I reach inside to get the registration? My license is in my back pocket."

The young cop gave a barely perceptible nod, and Deuce noted that his partner was now also exiting the squad car. His heart rate increased slightly, and he became aware of his breathing—it, too, sped up a little.

Leaning into the SUV he exchanged a look with Kaleem, and reached for the glovebox, opening it, and pulling out his registration paperwork. Standing upright once again, he handed it over.

"My license," he said. "It's in my wallet. In my back pocket."

"Yes. You mentioned. May I have it?" the young officer asked, evenly.

Deuce reached for his wallet, pulling it out slowly and fishing inside for his license and handing that over. He watched as the officer glanced at it, then at him; then at the license and finally, once again at him.

"Yeah, I know," he said. "I was trying to loc it for a minute. So, I look different. Gave up and ..." He ran a hand over his almost bald head.

Out of the corner of his eye, he noticed that the other officer had moved to the passenger side of the vehicle and was opening the door, beckoning for Kaleem to exit the SUV as well. Deuce felt his heartbeat speed up even more.

"We're going to ask you gentlemen to take a seat over here on the curb," the first cop said, his steely blue eyes meeting Deuce's.

Underlying the apprehension, Deuce felt the first threads of actual anger surface.

"You about to cuff us, too?" he asked.

The cop's eyes rose to his once again, but he said nothing.

"Nah," Deuce said slowly, maintaining eye contact. "Don't worry. I'm not 'refusing to comply'. Officer."

Sitting on their hands, Deuce and Kaleem watched as the younger of the two cops went through the routine, sitting in the driver's seat of the marked police vehicle, no doubt checking the tags, running background checks, searching for open warrants. His partner loomed a few feet behind them.

"You think he recognized your name?" Kaleem asked under his breath.

"I dunno," Deuce mumbled.

If either of the cops were Black, they would almost certainly recognize the name. *Christopher Scaife*, even with Jr. as an appellation, almost always raised eyebrows.

"At least that would explain this bullshit," Kaleem said.

"Hey. Both of you, shut the fuck up," the cop behind them ordered, sounding almost bored.

Deuce took a deep breath, forcing himself to remain calm.

He had been the one to beg his father for the new SUV. He saw a commercial while slouching on a dirty sofa in the basement at someone's party, drinking a warm beer. Half-asleep, he was planning on heading back to his dorm, but was too lazy to execute the plan. The sound was down on the television, and the channel was tuned to ESPN. A game was on, but he was just about the only one watching; and the room was crowded, noisy, and smelled like a mix of stale alcohol and even staler sweat. Two girls were hovering nearby, trying to get his attention by acting like they weren't interested in him at all.

And then the sleek, black SUV appeared, seeming to float across the screen. He sat upright. It did a couple of figure-8s on a wet pavement and lurched to a stop; the doors opened revealing the beautiful tan leather interior. Deuce felt something like love, and decided he had to have it. He was a little drunk, and not exactly alert. Now, he was inclined to believe that the way he felt about the Range Rover in that moment was kind of the way he often thought he felt about a girl he might pick up at two a.m. in a bar—that she was the most beautiful thing he had ever seen.

And like that girl from the bar, the Range Rover had turned out to be nice enough, pretty enough, but not quite as awe-inspiring as it appeared on that 65-inch screen in the basement of a party when he wasn't exactly sober. Now, it was more of a pain-in-the-ass than anything else. He'd had the damn thing three weeks and already been stopped twice. It was much too tricked-out and flashy for a sleepy college town in Pennsylvania.

When he got home for Christmas, he was leaving it at his father's house, and would drive the three-year old Beemer back to school, because this shit was just too stressful. The first traffic stop, he had actually been speeding, and had earned himself a two-hundred-dollar ticket. And right now, his ass was warming the curb instead of being warmed by the Range Rover's heated leather seats.

"Hey," the cop standing over him and Kaleem said. "I know you ..."

Here we go.

"You're Deuce Scaife."

He said nothing.

"Decided you didn't want to play for the Lions, huh? Even after going through all that trouble to dump your spot with the Fighting Irish?" There was a sardonic edge to the cop's voice, and a note of goading.

Deuce tried to think of what the least offensive thing to say would be. Penn State football fans weren't even like fans; they were more like a cult. Even more so since the sex abuse scandal rocked their world some years back. Now they were a doomsday cult—convinced that the world was conspiring against and persecuting them. And because of that, much, much more dangerous than your common garden-variety football cult. That kind he had encountered when he was a freshman at Notre Dame, along with a sustained campaign of hazing that made his mother insist—in a hysterical tirade—that his father get him transferred out of there after only one semester.

"Decided I didn't want to play football at all," Deuce said.

"How 'bout you, sport?" the cop seemed to be addressing Kaleem. "You play ball?" The cop gave a bitter laugh. "What am I sayin'? Of course you do."

Kaleem put his hands up as though in surrender. "Actually not, sir. Not a lick of athletic talent in me."

Deuce tried not to laugh. Kaleem was not only an excellent athlete, but the far superior sportsman between the two of them, as evidenced by the track-and-field scholarship that was giving him a full ride on tuition. That, and the fact that he was being looked at very seriously as a prospect for the 2020 Olympics.

"Yeah, right," the cop responded.

Because after all, in his world, two tall Black dudes in a nice ride had to be athletes. And Penn State athletes had a way of getting lots of favors, like nice cars to cruise around in on a Friday night. Strictly on loan of course. Because there were rules about stuff like that, and the last thing the school and boosters wanted to do after all that nasty Sandusky business was break any rules.

The first cop stepped out of the marked car and came striding back toward them. He extended a hand with Deuce's license and registration and when Deuce reached for them, let both drop onto the street.

"Thanks for your cooperation, gentlemen," he said. "Have a nice night."

He turned to walk away, leaving them sitting on the curb while his partner followed him back to the patrol car.

"YO, YOU *STILL* MAD?"

Deuce looked up at Kaleem who was tearing into a buffalo wing across the table, his lips, and fingers red and greasy from the sauce. "And you're not?"

"Nope. That shit used to happen to me practically on a daily back home in Oakland. And that was *without* the bad-ass whip."

"I don't know why we gotta live like that," Deuce mumbled, lifting his beer bottle to his lips.

"This is news to you? That we live like that? And you was mouthy as fuck by the way. That ain't the time to prove you got big balls. For real. You see the shit be happenin' out here?"

"Yeah, man. But ..." Deuce broke off, realizing that he was beginning to sound like a whiner. It was true, it wasn't news to him. But as a personal experience, yeah, it *was* new.

Back in New York, he was always insulated from all that. Growing up in a suburb where it was considered downright impolite to even acknowledge racial differences; and having the father he had, ensured that the only grit Deuce got exposed to was that which was manufactured for the music videos of his father's performing artists.

He had summered in the Hamptons, traveled extensively, and gotten VIP access to the hottest nightclubs in Manhattan before he even turned eighteen. But he didn't live under a rock. Of course, he knew cops got hard-ons for young Black men in decent rides. But never until just now had he experienced the apprehension and then the indignity of being pulled out of his car simply for driving while Black.

And even so, he knew that a little 'apprehension' was the best outcome. Many brothers out there weren't as lucky.

"You just need to take the edge off," Kaleem said. "Have you a little ..." He vaguely inclined his head in the direction of the bar, and Deuce turned to see what he was talking about. Three girls were sitting there, nursing drinks of their own and occasionally casting coy looks in Kaleem and his direction.

Deuce glanced at them and then did a double-take. One of the girls—the one who seemed least interested in looking over at either him or Kaleem—he recognized. Her name was Zora. She had been in his freshman African American Literature class and everyone had made much of the fact that she was named for the writer Zora Neale Hurston; and since then, she had just about lived up to her namesake. Now, she was a campus firebrand and flamethrower, who had helped organize a local Black Lives Matter chapter and seemed to be constantly on the look-out for her next boycott-and-protest opportunity.

On an average day, Deuce found her and the rest of that power-to-the-people crowd to be amusing; and on a bad day, annoying. Tonight though, he was curious. He wondered what she would say about his experiences over the last couple of weeks being stopped by the cops. She would probably tell him he should get used to it, and that it was convenient for him to finally start caring about it now that it happened to him. She might even give him a vaguely scornful look because he was wealthy, and was known to more than occasionally date White chicks.

"I'm not in the mood for all that right now," Deuce said, looking away from the trio of girls.

"A'ight. So just humor me," Kaleem said. "Because I am

definitely in the mood. Especially for that one honey, Zola, whatshername. With the bushy natural."

Deuce's head shot up. "Zora?"

"Yeah. Her. She fine as *fuck.*"

Deuce casually turned and looked over at the girls again. He hadn't thought of her that way before but, yeah … there was a little something about her.

Zora had a wild natural that looked like she basically woke up and yanked at it by the handful until it stood on end like the hair of that little Black character from that old show with all the kids, Little Ragamuffins, or something like that. And her skin was dark, and smooth as stone, with high prominent cheek-bones and full, plump lips. She didn't need the foundation that her two friends had plastered on because her complexion was dark enough to appear completely uniform, and there were few shades of lipstick that would successfully compete with the apparently natural dark plum hue. Her eyes were almost catlike in shape, but large and dark. Her nose was small but with flared nostrils that gave her a look of fierce determination.

"I think you better give up on that one, son. She's all about the struggle."

"Hell, black as I am? She's just looking for her African king, man. I think she messin' with that nigga, Rashad, but I just might be The One."

Deuce laughed despite himself. Kaleem *was* dark, though not as dark as Zora. And truth be told, it was that darkness, along with the movie-star white teeth and lean runner's body that probably got Kaleem so much play. He was handsome enough probably—Deuce didn't feel equipped to assess other dudes' looks—but there was something about Kaleem that drew women to him in droves. Mostly blonde chicks, often athletes themselves. Kal sometimes partook of those delights, as did he, but his friend had a definite and strong preference for the sisters.

In college, anything goes, man, Kal had told him once. *But once I graduate I'm marrying a queen and building a Black nation. Four, maybe five little Kaleems. Nah mean?*

Deuce *didn't* know what he meant. Because he wasn't thinking about nation-building at all. He was thinking about enjoying life; and as a secondary goal, getting the degree that meant so much to both his parents. The rest of it, he would figure out as he went along.

"G'on invite them over, then," Deuce offered.

"You sure?" Kaleem asked, licking buffalo sauce off his fingers. "You can't just sit here though, man. You gotta keep the conversation goin' with her girls while I do my thing."

"Yeah, I got you."

Kaleem didn't ask twice. He slid out of the booth and with complete confidence strode across the crowded bar in the direction of the three girls. In the meantime, Deuce looked down at his phone, whose face had lit up with an incoming text message.

It was his mother, confirming that he still planned to drive up that weekend for the Christmas holiday, and asking whether he wanted her to ask his father to send someone.

Deuce responded, telling her that he preferred to drive. He didn't mention why, or tell her that he planned to leave the Range Rover when he came back. She would have a fit if he told her he was stopped, and probably want to call someone up to complain. His mother was fiercely protective and never shy about name-dropping and throwing around her connection to his father if she thought that would get her the result she wanted. He loved her, but that shit was embarrassing.

"You all know my boy, Deuce, right?"

He looked up at Kaleem who had escorted the three girls over, two of them giggling as he extended a hand.

"This is Sophie ..." Pretty with long, auburn hair that was most likely not hers, and hazel eyes that may or may not be her real eye-color. "And Mia ..." Much prettier than Sophie with shoulder-length black curls and a cute gap-toothed smile. "And Zora."

Deuce shook each of their hands in turn and mumbled a brief 'hello' as Zora slid into the booth next to him and Mia at the end, next to her. Kaleem let Sophie into the booth before him on the other side, which was what Deuce assumed his friend wanted, so he could he could be sitting directly opposite Zora.

"You ladies want something to drink?" Kaleem offered, waving for a waitperson.

Mia and Sophie readily agreed, but Zora demurred, with that low, almost husky voice that Deuce recalled from her campus speeches and comments in class, could be quite powerful when she wanted it to be. Tonight, she sounded quieter and more reserved, like she wanted to be anyplace but here. He could relate.

"What y'all up to tonight?" Mia asked.

The way she leaned forward when she did, made it clear she was directing the question mainly to Kaleem. When Zora turned to look at her friend, her hair brushed the side of Deuce's face, because it was so close in the booth. It was coarse but soft at the same time, and bore the vague scent of fruit. Beneath the table, her thigh was touching his, though barely. She seemed to realize that at the same time he did, because she shifted slightly, and just enough so that they were no longer making contact, but not enough that it would appear she was recoiling from him.

Deuce inhaled, wanting to smell her hair again, wondering whether he could identify precisely what fruit the scent was.

"I heard the Nupes got somethin' goin' on," Kaleem said. "Y'all wan' ride?"

Mia and Sophie said *'yes'* in unison just as Zora said, *'no thanks.'*

The table fell quiet for a moment. "You sure?" Kaleem said, addressing Zora directly, as though her girls hadn't even spoken.

"I'm sure," Zora returned. "I roll out tomorrow and I still haven't done any packing."

"I could help you with that," Kaleem said. He grinned and then bit into his lower lip.

Next to Deuce, Zora's shoulders shook a little as she gave a brief laugh. "Thank you, but no. I can't imagine letting anyone see my messy-ass room right now."

Like the voice of someone who had just woken up and not yet cleared their throat—that's what her voice sounded like. But smoother, warmer. Sexier.

Deuce cleared his throat now, almost guilty at the thought. Kaleem had his eye on this one, so he had no business thinking about how sexy she did or didn't sound.

And besides, she wasn't his type. He liked Spanish chicks. Long dark hair, caramel complexions, and just enough African blood in them to give them ass for days. He liked that they were emotive and a little wild, that they fucked as hard as they fought ... all stereotypes, it was true, but in his experience, also based in a *little* bit of fact.

"Zora always tryin' to break up a party," Mia said, her voice a little bitter.

Clearly, she wasn't mad that Zora wouldn't be going to the Nupe party so much as she was that Kaleem would choose to skip it as well, just to hang with Zora.

"Ain't nobody breakin' up the party," Kaleem said. "We can still roll. We'll just drop Zora off on the way." He turned his smile, and his charm in Mia's direction.

Fickle muthafucka, Deuce thought, amused.

"I think I'ma sit this one out, too, man," he said.

"D. C'mon."

"Take the truck, just bring it back clean."

Kaleem looked at him with narrowed eyes for a moment then shook his head, a look of realization entering his eyes before he nodded. "Okay, cool."

"You're not coming?" This from Sophie.

"Not feelin' it tonight," Deuce said, trying to sound apologetic.

"We had a little run-in with law enforcement earlier," Kaleem explained. "I think my boy was traumatized."

"Really? What happened?" This time it was Zora who spoke.

"Zora's going to represent you in your civil rights action against the police department," Sophie said.

"It wasn't a big deal," Deuce said, angling his body to face Zora as much as he could in the confines of the booth. "We just got stopped that's all."

"Were you speeding?" Zora asked. She had turned to face him as well. Her eyes, he now saw, were a lot less dark than he thought. They were visibly brown, though not quite light-brown, and fringed by long lashes that curled almost sharply upward at the ends.

"Nope."

"Broken taillight?"

"Nah."

"So, it was one of those stops, huh? That's the worst kind." Zora shook her head. "When you're pretty sure you haven't done anything wrong and there you are … at the mercy of someone with all the power, and questionable motives."

Deuce shrugged.

"I'm sorry that happened to you," she said, so low that only he could hear her.

"Who wants in on some more wings?" Kaleem asked loudly from the other side of the table.

Deuce broke his gaze away from Zora's. "I could eat some wings," he said. Then he looked at her. "How 'bout you?"

"Always down for wings," she said, smiling.

"THANKS FOR THE RIDE."

They were in front of Zora's dorm, and she was preparing to get out of the SUV when Deuce had an impulse. He could escape too. He still didn't want to go to the Kappa party, and his dorm was mere yards away.

"You're welcome," he said.

He turned and looked over his shoulder as he spoke and his eyes met Zora's for a moment. She smiled at him, a little quirk at the corner of her full lips.

After she heard about his traffic stop, Zora had been much more talkative, and when she did speak, Deuce felt the vibration of her voice. That it could be so low, and yet so feminine was a puzzle. Once she loosened up, they wound up talking about all kinds of random stuff including what she called her "latest obsession"—a baking reality show where teams competed to make the best and most creative cupcakes. Deuce didn't give a crap about reality shows, no matter their subject. But he liked listening to and watching her talk about them. She was a "hand-talker," once even accidentally hitting him on the side of the face as she gestured to make her point. Laughing, she'd touched his cheek briefly and apologized. Deuce thought he felt her skin on his long after she removed her hand.

"Enjoy the packing," Kaleem said, glancing toward the back of the car.

The dismissiveness in his voice confirmed for Deuce that his friend's attentions had been transferred elsewhere. Kal wasn't used to working for it, so he had no patience for a prolonged chase.

"Hey," Deuce said, as Zora opened the door. "Hold up a sec."

She shut it again without getting out, looking at him questioningly.

"Might as well jump out here myself. Kaleem, don't mess up my ride, man. I'm serious."

"I'll treat it like it's my own," Kaleem said, stroking the arm-rest. "Now get the hell out my car."

Mia and Sophie laughed, as though it was funniest thing they had ever heard, though Sophie shot Deuce a long, significant look as well.

"Last chance," she sang. And Deuce knew she wasn't just talking about his chance to opt into going to the party.

Shaking his head, he unlocked his seatbelt and shut off the engine, sliding out of the SUV and leaving the door open for Kaleem.

On the same side, in the rear, Zora opened the door and stepped out, pulling the collar of her coat up to her ears. The coat was knee-length, one of those puffy ones that made people look like walking grenades. With it, she was wearing close-fitting jeans and brown UGGs that were splotchy and mud-stained; not something a girl wore for a night out with her friends, even in college. Zora had probably been lured out of her dorm when her only plans were to pack for Winter Break.

When Kaleem came around and jumped into the driver's

seat, he shut the door and waved out of the window, pulling off without another word. Deuce and Zora looked at each other and laughed.

"I think you might have made a mistake," she said.

"Nah," Deuce said, smiling at her. "I'm pretty sure I didn't."

"I mean, a mistake letting him have your car. Your really nice car, I might add."

"Kal's good," Deuce said. "He only *acts* a fool."

Zora shrugged. "Okay. If you say so."

They both stood there for a few silent moments, until finally she inclined her head in the direction of her dorm. "You want to come in?"

Zora's room was a corner unit, with two large windows that overlooked the lawn behind the dorm. When she shoved open the door and flipped on the lights, the windows were the first thing Deuce noticed. The godawful mess was the second.

"Wow," he laughed. "You weren't lyin' huh?"

Zora laughed with him. "Nope. I warned you that it's a mess. I have a lot of cleaning on top of all the packing to do."

She had a nice laugh. Delicate, soft, with a hint of the same huskiness that made her speaking voice so unique.

"But you still let me see it," he said. "I feel special."

Shrugging, Zora tossed her handbag across the room and onto her bed. "You're welcome."

"Where are you from?" he asked, on a whim.

"Ahm, New Jersey," she said, looking amused.

"No. I mean ..."

She cocked her head to one side, waiting for him to go on. "You mean ...what?"

"You just look ..."

"I look ..." she prompted him again, looking close to laughter.

"Not just American. You look ..."

"African?" she finished for him. She shut the door and leaned against it, that little half-smile crossing her lips again. "You can say it. It's not like it's an insult. I *am* African. My father is Senegalese."

"I didn't mean ..."

"Oh, just ... shut up," she said.

She grabbed the front of his coat and pulled him against her, getting up on her toes and pressing her full, plum-colored lips against his.

TWO

Nah. Hell nah.

He was being punked. That was the only way to explain this. Out of the almost one hundred thousand students at Penn State... No way.

Deuce took a deep breath and stood as Zora approached his table in the Hub. Wearing a scowl with her grey sweatshirt and jeans, she was obviously just as surprised and dismayed as he.

"Wow," she said, her tone sardonic. "Small world."

"That wasn't your name," he said. "On Zimride, the person who responded wasn't you."

"I had a friend find the ride for me," Zora said, referring to his inquiry on the campus rideshare system. "I didn't know it was you either. Obviously."

"Doesn't that defeat the purpose?" he asked sourly. "Of knowing exactly who you're letting into your car? Of knowing exactly whose car you're getting into?"

"Look," Zora said. "We don't have to do this. If you're uncomfortable, I'm sure I can find someone else."

"Like who? It's five days before Christmas. And didn't you tell me last week you were leaving the next day? But I guess that wasn't true either."

"Either? When did I ever lie to … whatever, man. For your information, I planned to leave when I said I would. But then my car died on me. But you wouldn't know anything about that, being that those are poor people problems and all."

Deuce ignored the jab. "So, we doing this or not? I want to make it to Jersey before nightfall."

Zora shrugged. "Then let's go."

It was only then that Deuce noticed the heavy duffle she had slung over her right shoulder, along with the smaller weekend bag and pocketbook in her left hand. He reached for it and after a moment's hesitation, Zora surrendered the weighty bag.

Without a word, Deuce headed for the exit, sensing her presence just behind him.

Three-and-a-half hours. That was how long it would take to drive from State College to Short Hills, New Jersey. He could endure almost anything for three-and-a-half hours. Even the company of the one girl on campus he least wanted to see.

What he'd been hoping for when he posted the rideshare inquiry was just someone to kill the miles and hours with, someone he could shoot the breeze with about music, or if it was a dude, football. Maybe they would share some mutual hatred of the New England Pats, or talk about how overrated Cam Newton was. The last thing he wanted to do was relive his brief misadventure with the campus revolutionary.

When they got to his car, Deuce disengaged the locks and tossed Zora's bag in the backseat of the Range Rover with his stuff and turned to face her again.

"Here," he said, reaching for the smaller bags. "Lemme put those back here as well, so you'll have some legroom."

"Thanks." She handed them over willingly.

Once he'd tossed those bags in the backseat as well and straightened up, Deuce was surprised to find that she was still standing there, next to the passenger-side door, shifting her weight from one leg to the other, as though trying to keep warm in the frigid air.

"It's open," he said inclining his head in the direction of the door.

Zora looked at him blankly, and Deuce rolled his eyes, opening it for her, waiting for her to get in and then shutting it. Taking a deep breath, he walked around the rear of the car and got in on his side.

"Your tank is full," Zora noted when he started the engine.

"Yeah. So what?"

"The deal on Zimride was that the passenger pays for gas, you pay tolls."

"I don't need it," Deuce shrugged.

"It doesn't matter if you need it. It's the principle."

"And we know you're all about principles," he said as he pulled away from the curb.

"I COULD'VE SWORN you said you lived in New York."

Zora had removed her boots and curled her feet beneath her. Deuce tried not to look at her legs in the close-fitting jeans. Unless he was mistaken, they were the same jeans from that night. That dumb-ass night that he couldn't stop thinking about.

"I do. Upstate. My father lives in Jersey. I'm going there first to see him, my stepmother, my baby brother and sister, and to spend the night with them."

"How many siblings do you have?"

Deuce looked at her, and Zora shrugged.

"Is that something I should know?" she asked.

Maybe not. Some other chick, maybe. But not Zora. Of all the girls unlikely to have followed his complicated blended family's exploits on the entertainment blogs, Zora was probably the unlikeliest.

"Four. Two brothers, two sisters."

"And you're the eldest?"

"Yup."

Zora breathed a deep sigh. "Chris ..."

"Deuce. I don't like to be called Chris. That's my father's name."

Out of the corner of his eye, Deuce saw her take another breath.

"Sorry," she said. "I get it. Your father is a big presence. You want to be your own person."

"Zora, don't ... psychoanalyze me."

"Sorry," she said again. "Look ..." She touched his thigh. "Can we just ... clean the slate and ...?"

"Clean the slate?" he repeated.

"Yeah. I mean, look ... it's not as though it wouldn't have always gone down exactly the way it did. It's just that I was the one to put it into action, and ..."

"You're doing it again. Trying to head-shrink me. You don't know how it would've gone down, Zora."

"Of course I do. Do you even know your rep on campus?"

"Nah," he said sarcastically. "Why don't you tell me about it?"

"I could," Zora said. "But I don't want us to start fighting again."

"You don't think I can take it?" Deuce, switched lanes, heading toward the I-80 on-ramp.

"I'm sure you can take it. I'm just not sure I want to be the one to dish it out."

"Go ahead. We have three hours to kill."

"Okay ... but don't say you didn't ..."

"Just spit it out."

"You're Chris Scaife's son. Born with a silver spoon in your mouth, and grew up in a little post-racial bubble. You're from that crowd who says color doesn't matter because the only one that matters where you grew up is green. You date White chicks almost exclusively and pretend that doesn't matter either, and sisters like me you hardly ever give a second glance. Which might be insulting, but for the fact that you treat those poor little White girls with nothing resembling respect, and are pretty much done with them after a week. So ... there you have it. Truth."

Deuce shook his head, and shook off the pang in his chest as well. "Wow ... now that was some angry Black woman bull-shit right there."

"See what I mean? White chicks don't get angry too? Or is it just us you don't like to see mad? But come to think of it, the ones you mess with don't get angry, do they? They just line up, one after the other to get their turn with Christopher Scaife Jr."

"You forget what happened between you and me that night? I didn't see you walking away from your ... turn."

"Okay, I'll give you that. But I chose it, Deuce. You didn't choose me. I wanted you. But it was sexual curiosity, that's all. And that's all it was for you, too. Admit it. I'm probably the blackest chick you've seen naked since ... ever. You're just mad I was the one to shut it down afterwards."

"That's one fucked up double-standard. You see that right? And I ain't about all that color-struck nonsense."

"Really."

"Yeah. Really."

"And how is what I said a double-standard?"

"Do you like to be dismissed, Zora?"

"I don't know. I can't say it's ever happened."

"Well that's what all that mess you just said is—dismissal. You don't even know me. And that night I thought ..." Deuce stopped talking abruptly, realizing he was on the brink of sounding like he was begging. And that was something he would not do.

Zora said nothing for a long while, and when she finally spoke, her voice was different. "You thought what?"

"We started talking about the traffic stop," Deuce said. "Remember? That's why we started talking. And then when I went to your dorm, we talked some more. The shit that went down later ..."

"The shit that went down later ..." she prompted. "Go on."

That's not why I was there, he wanted to but did not say.

He was there because when he and Zora talked in the bar, their voices slightly raised so they could hear over the din, he'd forgotten that they weren't alone. Kaleem and her girls Mia and Sophie might as well have not been there. And then when Zora said she had to go back to pack for her drive home the next day for Christmas Break, Deuce hadn't wanted her to go, so he went with her.

The idea of ending the evening at yet another party with Kaleem and some girls who were pretending they didn't care who he was, but clearly did, seemed intolerable. He just wanted to hang with Zora, to talk some more, to listen to that warm voice of hers, to smell that unidentified fruity scent in her hair, to have an excuse to examine her dark-as-night skin and stare into her cat-like eyes.

He just wanted to be with her.

And that was something in his entire time at Penn State,

Deuce could not recall having happened before—that he wanted to be with a girl just for the pleasure of her company.

Then in her room—her messy-as-hell room—Zora had jumped him.

There was no other way to put it. As soon as the door was shut, she turned and kissed him, and he went with it. How could he not go with it? Her lips were soft, full and tasted like the illegally-consumed beer they'd been drinking all night. Her chest was soft against his, and she grabbed his hands to place them on her ass, pressing her pelvis forward and reaching down to stroke his hardness.

This girl wants me? he recalled thinking. *This girl ... wants* me.

The thought was surprising only because if anyone had asked him before then, he would have said that few were the girls who did not. But Zora wasn't just any girl. She was the girl Kaleem would have called a queen; she was a warrior. She had consequence and purpose. She was not the kind of girl who generally wanted him.

Except that night, she did. And no lie, that shit was off the chain. He grabbed handfuls of her thick, coarse hair in his fists, and they screwed with the lights on, her eyes locked with his, her powerful, firm thighs gripping his hips, holding him tight against her. This wasn't some fumbling, grappling half-drunken college dorm encounter. This was grown-ass lovemaking, like a man and woman were meant to have. Deuce was present for every breath, every groan, every kiss, and the ultimate collapse of their damp bodies against each other.

Afterwards, he fell asleep. He slept hard and deep until Zora shook him gently awake and he sat up, dazed and momentarily unsure of his surroundings. Her room was clean and she was almost completely packed. Smiling at him once she saw he was awake, Zora had shoved the sheets aside, lifted the hem of the long t-shirt she was wearing and revealed that there was absolutely nothing underneath.

Deuce left after that, in a daze, exhausted and idly considering whether he might look her up while he was home. Zora had kissed him goodbye at her door, told him to enjoy Winter Break. All the way to his dorm, walking in the cold, he couldn't stop licking his lips, like some of her just might be there for him to taste.

The very next day, he ran into her girl Sophie, and when he asked her if he could have Zora's number, she looked confused.

Why d'you need her number? she said. *She's still on campus. Go see her.*

Confused, Deuce did exactly that. She was on campus? Whatever happened to driving home for Break? She said she had no finals, just final papers, and so she could leave early. She'd cleaned her room, she'd packed ...

As luck would have it, Zora was in her dorm's common room when Deuce walked in. She was sitting on a sofa with her feet up on a coffee table, and next to her was a brother with shoulder-length locs. Zora had a bright orange scarf tied in her hair, the color accentuating her complexion in a way that was almost breathtaking. She, and her companion were laughing about something, something that was obviously very, very funny.

Mid-laugh, Zora turned and spotted him. A momentary look of surprise crossed her features, her eyebrows lifting for a second. And very casually, she lifted a hand in a wave. Then Zora returned to her conversation, never giving him a second glance.

"DEUCE."

He looked at her. She was chewing on her lower lip and looking away from him, out the window at the nondescript miles of highway.

"What?"

"I have an idea. And I don't want you to shoot it down. I want you to think about it, okay?"

Deuce mumbled something unintelligible.

"Will you think about it?"

"Yeah."

"But before I tell you my idea I have a tiny confession."

At that Deuce looked at her again.

"I knew it was you," she said. "That was offering the ride. I knew it was you, and I asked Mia to respond because I wasn't sure you'd want to ride with me."

Deuce forced himself not to smile. "So that look you gave me back at the Hub ..."

"Best acting I've done all year," she admitted.

"It wasn't all that good," he lied.

Zora punched him in the arm. "Shut up. You didn't know."

"Nah, I didn't know," he said. Their eyes met and held for so long that Zora blushed, her gaze dropping to her lap. Good thing too, since he might have run off the road otherwise.

Deuce wanted to ask her why she'd pretended, but he knew. As much as she was outside of his comfort zone, he was probably way out of hers as well.

"What's your idea?" he asked instead.

"I was thinking that maybe ..." Zora sighed deeply. "That we could pretend that night didn't happen. And just ... begin again."

"I don't want to pretend that night never happened," Deuce said right away. "But, I do want to ..."

"Begin again?" she said, that warm husky voice of hers lowering even more.

Damn, she was sexy as hell.

"Yeah," he said. "Let's do that."

Zora turned in her seat and extended a hand. Deuce took it. It was small and warm. He didn't want to let it go.

"Nice to meet you," she said. "I'm Zora Diallo."

THREE

Deuce woke up to a stiff neck and back, and the blaring, aggressive cheerfulness of a Disney movie theme song. Opening his eyes, he realized he'd fallen asleep in the home theater, and now it was morning. On the carpeted floor, a few feet away, his baby brother Landyn was walking around in circles, wearing only a diaper and t-shirt, babbling nonsensically, and shaking his bottle like a pint-sized dictator.

A few feet away, his sister Jasmin was drawing something, her brows furrowed in concentration. And Kaden, his other brother was watching the movie, sitting so close to the screen, he had to let his head fall all the way back to look up at it.

Staggering to his feet, Deuce walked over to Kaden and smacked him on the side of the head.

"Too close, man," he said. "Move on back to the seats."

Kaden, eyes still glued to the screen, got up and backed himself into the front row, collapsing into one of the extra-wide, plush seats that had been Deuce's bed for the evening.

Still circling and trying to loosen his neck, Deuce wandered out of the theater and down the hallway toward the foyer. He hadn't made it to his actual bed the night before, but planned to do so right now. First, he would have to call his mother. He hadn't given her the heads-up that he was planning to stay at his father's place, and had no doubt she was going to give him the business.

But he'd had a change of plans once Zora came over. After Christmas dinner with his mom, aunts and grandmother, he'd driven more than an hour to Jersey and visited with the rest of his family for a while. He gave the kids their gifts and spent some time playing with his siblings, then finally admitted to himself why he'd come in the first place. Zora lived only about fifteen miles from his father's house.

What you up to? he'd asked when he called her.

Not much. Hanging out.

Come hang out here.

Come get me, she said.

And so, he had.

Now, on his way up to his bedroom suite, Deuce bumped into his stepmother, heading downstairs, a bounce in her step.

"Your Dad called your mother last night," Robyn said. "Let her know you were with us, and that you're okay. But you should probably call her yourself once you've had a chance to eat something."

"Yup."

Robyn ran a hand over his head as he passed her. "And maybe get a haircut while you're here? Your father's going in a little while. You can tag along with him."

"Yeah. I will."

Deuce made his way to the bedroom suite that was his whenever he stayed at his father's place. It used to be the master, but when Robyn and his dad got married, she moved them down to the other end of the hall to what used to be one of the guest suites, because it was closer to the kids' rooms and on the sunnier side of the house overlooking the pool. That cleared the way for Deuce to luck up and get a space that was equivalent in size to a small apartment.

After he laid it on thick with Robyn about the need for someplace quiet and private to study, and to just get away from the hectic noise of the household, she had convinced his father to let him get it decorated. Now it was laid out like an apartment, with a distinct bedroom, separated from the living room where he had even managed to get the decorators to include a mini-bar, cleverly concealed in a credenza.

Once he saw the completed renovations, his father had looked at Deuce and smirked.

You need peace and quiet to study, huh?

And the very next day, someone had come to remove the lock on the main door to the suite, and even the one separating the living from the bedroom. His father had never explicitly prevented him from having female guests, and so Deuce often had. But the only people he was guaranteed to keep out were his younger siblings, because they hadn't yet figured out that his authority didn't carry the same weight as that of their parents. His father and Robyn on the other hand, were live threats to him getting too carried away with anyone he might invite upstairs.

Last night, he hadn't invited Zora up, but when the kids went to bed he led her to the home theater. The house was quiet and secure; the dinner guests were gone and the house-guests in their rooms. Though it was only about ten-thirty, everyone was bushed from the long day. Christmas "dinner" at his father's house usually started as brunch and continued until eight–thirty or so when there were drinks and dessert; and then another hour of socializing on the patio.

It's hard for a man to be sexy and funny at the same time,

Zora said, while she watched Jaime Foxx onscreen. *But he pulls it off sometimes.*

He watched the movie with her only half-heartedly at first, because he was dying to touch her, dying to kiss her. But she wasn't giving out those signals and about an hour in, he gave up and watched the movie, pulling Zora's legs to rest across his lap.

Around eleven-fifty, Zora caught sight of the time, let loose a curse, and told him she had to get home. So, Deuce drove her, a tight, dull ache at his groin that didn't ease up until he had dropped her off and was on his way back to the house. When he got there, he grabbed a couple of beers from the patio bar, some leftovers from the kitchen, started another movie and watched it until he fell asleep.

AFTER A QUICK SHOWER, Deuce headed back downstairs to the patio where his stepmother and the kids had assembled for breakfast. The other houseguests, Robyn's brother and his woman, and her mother with her gentleman friend had not yet made an appearance. Just as he was about to sit, his father came in, grabbed a waffle from the table, and said he was heading out to get his hair cut.

"You comin'?" he asked Deuce.

Nodding, he shoveled a forkful of eggs into his mouth and followed his father out to the front. When they were standing in front of the car, Deuce was surprised to have the keys tossed his way.

"You drive. I feel like riding today."

They pulled out of the driveway, Deuce aware of his father's eyes on him as he maneuvered the Maybach through the wrought iron gates.

"How's school?"

He shrugged. "You know."

"No, I *don't* know," his father said. "Unless you tell me."

"It's cool. Nothing to report."

"Nothing to report, huh? You know I only ask because ..."

"I know." Deuce said. "Because of last time."

'Last time' was his nightmarish first semester of freshman year at Notre Dame where apparently, even before he arrived, a few people had been nursing a fair amount of resentment that someone like him—from a family that was more than well-off—had scored a full scholarship to play football. It was the first time Deuce could remember his father's name being a drawback instead of a considerable benefit.

At his first day at practice—which was late in the summer, even before classes started—his welcome gift was a literal pile of shit in his locker. And it went on from there. His gear was mysteriously misplaced, his cleats damaged, the numbers ripped from his jersey ... and that was only in addition to the almost constant barrage of daily slights and insults.

But he was willing to ride it out, because if you played the game, you knew football culture was different. You didn't whine to the coach because someone was delivering hard knocks, whether on or off the field. Deuce knew that if he manned up, handled it, and never complained, he would eventually earn the respect of his teammates, most of whom weren't participating in the hazing, but just watching it from the sidelines to see how he coped.

Then in a moment of frustration, he mentioned an incident —that one involving two dead mice hanging by their necks in his locker—to his mother. And in a way that was completely unlike her, she had gradually and gently teased out the full story of the harassment that had been going on since he arrived on campus. She listened, and said very little.

The next thing Deuce knew, his father was calling him to

ask how he was, and what he wanted to do. Together, they agreed he would ride it out, but that if it should ever get to a point where he wanted to quit, he'd be the one to call it.

That wasn't good enough for his mother.

Not even two days after the call with his father, his mother was on a plane headed to South Bend, Indiana. And one day after that, she had withdrawn Deuce from the university, making a huge stink in the process.

I shouldna never *trusted your ass to take care of this!* she screamed at his father on the phone when they were back in New York. *You think I'ma let my kid go to college to be abused by folks?*

Once her tirade was over, Deuce had a separate conversation with his father. But if he thought he was about to be comforted for his ordeal, he had another think coming.

What did we decide?

That I would stick it out, and …

So why are you back home? Did you change your mind?

Nah! But Ma …

You're not her little boy anymore, Deuce, his father said. *You decide. And stand up for yourself! Be respectful to her, always. But you decide as a man. You hear me? Don't let that shit happen again.*

It was a lesson he never forgot, and hell he was only eighteen at the time. But after a lifetime of placating his mother to avoid her flying off the handle, the decision to leave Notre Dame hadn't been a hard one. And once he walked away, and because of the *way* he walked away, going back hadn't been an option.

So, with only two weeks before the start of the second semester of freshman year, strings had been pulled to get him into Penn State. If he wanted to play ball, he would have to be a walk-on, but it was implied that he would be very welcome on the team. The program had lost a lot of talent in recent years and the school wasn't the football player magnet that it used to be, so Deuce could have played. But he didn't want to.

Though he had always liked playing ball, he had never *loved* playing ball.

"School is a'ight," he said now, a little more forcefully. "It's all good."

"*All* good?"

"Yeah, man. It's good. Although ..."

"Although ...?"

He looked away from the road for a moment to glance at his father who was staring him down in that way he had. Chris Scaife Sr. was the only person whose stares made him feel like he was about to be found out, and called out. Even when he hadn't done anything wrong.

"I think I might leave the Range Rover home and take the Beemer."

At this, his father turned around in his seat, his scrutiny even more intense. "Why?"

"I don't know. Maybe it's ... you know, too much."

"You damn near begged for that car ..."

"I know."

"... and I didn't even want to get it ..."

"I *know.*"

"And now you want to what? Park it under a tree in my driveway and take the *old* whip?"

"It's not that old," Deuce mumbled.

"That's bullshit. What happened?"

Sighing, Deuce allowed the whole story to come spilling out. "I don't want to be attracting that kind of negative attention," he concluded. "It ain't even worth it. I mean, I like the car, but ..."

"Wait. Don't tell me you're that soft."

"I ain't hardly *soft*," Deuce said, bristling at the suggestion. "I just don't need to set myself up to be a target."

His father laughed. "I hate to break it to you, man. But life already did that. When you were born Black and a male, *that's* what set you up. That's something you ain't gon' be able to shed, no matter what car you drive."

"And I wouldn't want to!"

"Well *that's* a relief," his father said.

"You know what? I'm tired of people actin' like I don' know what it means to be a Black man just because I'm rich."

"But you're not rich. You have nothing. *I'm* rich."

Deuce sucked his teeth. "Whatever, man."

His father laughed and clapped him on the shoulder. "Okay. You know what? I'ma give it to you like this: that Range Rover is *your* muthafuckin' ride. *Drive it.* Don't let anyone intimidate you into being other than who you are. So you're young, rich and Black. They don't like it? Fuck 'em."

Deuce tried, but couldn't prevent the smile from breaking free. His father hardly ever cussed when he spoke to him, but when he did, it was only when one or two things was true: *one; Robyn wasn't around to hear it, and two; he was giving things to him straight.*

"I mean it. Drive your car. Don't be stupid, don't be arrogant. But don't let them break you down either."

Deuce said nothing.

"You hear me?"

He felt his father's large hand on the back of his neck.

"Yeah," he said. "I hear you."

"So, what's up with you and this new chick you brought around? What's her name again?"

"Zora," Deuce said. He didn't know why, but just saying her name made him want to cheese.

"*Zora.* Nice. So ..."

"Just a friend."

"Uh huh." His father sounded unconvinced.

"Yeah. I mean, she's just … different."

"Different, huh?"

Deuce glanced at his father out of the corner of his eye and noted the smirk on his face, but pretended not to, instead refocusing only on the road ahead.

———

"WAIT. Didn't I just see you last night?"

Phone up against his ear, Deuce watched from the other side of the barbershop as his father got the finishing touches on his shave. His own haircut had been done for a little while, and when he got tired of the shit-talking and sports predictions, he called Zora. Just to see what was up with her since they hadn't talked after he dropped her off the evening before.

"Yeah. Damn. Just checking to see if you're a'ight. Is that a problem?"

"Why wouldn't I be alright? From what I remember, you saw me walk up my front path, unlock the door and step right into my house, didn't you? I know, because I waved at you from the open front door."

He smiled. He kind of liked it when she teased him.

"I'm a gentleman. I was taught to wait until the lady was safe before pulling off. And there's been a few home invasion robberies in Jersey so you never know."

Zora laughed her husky yet melodious laugh. "Well, no one's invaded *my* home. So I'm totally fine. But thanks for checking."

"You're welcome."

For a few moments, there was silence between them. Across the room, the barber was wiping his father's face clean.

Soon he would take out his powder and brush and Deuce would no longer have the privacy he needed to seal this deal.

"What're you doin' later?"

"Nothing. The usual for when it's cold as hell outside. Netflix. Chill."

Deuce grinned. "Come do that with me."

"Why, when I could do it right here? And not even have to change out of my PJs."

"You haven't changed out of your PJs?"

"Nope." Zora made a popping noise with her lips when she pronounced the word.

"That's nasty."

She laughed. "I showered before bed."

"Yeah. Sure you did."

"I *did*."

"Deuce!"

He looked up. His father was done, and beckoning for him as he doled out tips to the barber and his assistant.

"If you don't want to come over, let me come over there then."

"I probably *should* leave the house," Zora said, almost as though talking to herself. "Whenever I try to veg out all day, it seems like a good idea, and then around seven-thirty I start feeling a little stir-crazy."

"So ... you comin' over or ...?"

"Ahm ..."

Deuce stood, deliberately slow-walking toward the exit of the barbershop where his father was waiting for him. Ducking his head, and lowering his voice, he spoke deliberately softly into the phone.

"C'mon, Zee. I want to see you."

The nickname, and the way he'd laid it all out there seemed to have startled her into silence. It kind of startled him as well.

Deuce removed the phone from his ear and looked at it to make sure the connection hadn't been broken. "You there?"

"Yeah. I'm here." Her voice sounded more sober, and much less playful.

"Can I see you?" he repeated.

"Okay."

"I'll be there in an hour and a half. Pack a swimsuit and a change of clothes."

"A swim ..."

"Yeah. A swimsuit. And something to wear after. See you in ninety minutes."

"But Deuce, it's forty degr..."

"Yeah, I know. 'Bye."

HOLDING her phone between her shoulder and the side of her head, Zora stuffed her black one-piece swimsuit and a brown viscose skirt into her hobo along with an orange scarf and a long-sleeved beige t-shirt.

"You talk to Rashad since you've been home?" the voice on the other end of the line asked.

"Nope. He hit me up a couple of times, but I didn't pick up. All we have right now to talk about at the moment is business, and I'm on Break, so ..."

"Yeah, but you guys barely even broke up. After two years being together, that's kind of cold to cut a brother off like that. And I can't believe you're going to hang out with Deuce Scaife again."

"Mia," Zora sighed. "It's no big deal. I'm just ..."

"Trying to get a little of that good-good," her friend cackled on the other end of the line. "I don't blame you, girl. Nothing like it to get you over the post-relationship hump. No pun intended. And if what I hear about him is true ..."

Oh, it was definitely *true.* But Mia didn't need to know all that.

"Mia, I'll call you back when I get home later. And please stop bringing up Rashad. He is definitely past tense."

"If you say so. But dudes like Rashad don't come a dime-a-dozen. You should ..."

Zora held the phone away from her ear.

She had heard this sermon one time too many for her taste —about how Rashad was a "woke brother", how he was on some "Barack Obama-type shit" and most of all how *rare* he was. That was the kind of talk that helped lead Zora into such an intense relationship with him so quickly in the first place; and it was probably also responsible for her staying in said relationship for at least one year too long.

It was just that the optics of her and Rashad were too powerful to ignore. People loved the *idea* of them. Together, they looked like the prototype of the ideal Black power couple —her with the dark skin and big natural, and Rashad, with his militant bearing and unrelenting scowl, staring down anyone who dared to look at him even halfway funny. And that they were co-chairs and co-founders of a Black Lives Matter chapter? That just made it even more of a modern Black American storybook romance.

When she was honest with herself, Zora admitted that it wasn't just other people who loved the idea of her and Rashad. She had too. Until just a few months ago, she was as bought into the story as anyone else. Breaking it off had actually given her a few anxiety attacks. What if he was The One? What if she was being foolish by letting him go?

There was no question Rashad was going to be making some big moves in the next few years. He was the guy who would miss his five-year college reunion, but only because he was running for State Senate, or was a nationally-respected activist too busy to attend since he was on a speaking tour. But being in love with Rashad's passion and drive; being enamored of his politics, and in sync with his worldview wasn't the same as being in love, enamored with or in sync with Rashad himself. It had taken Zora a long time to acknowledge that, and now she was determined not to backslide by having anyone persuade her otherwise. She had been avoiding his calls mostly because of all the people who might attempt that persuasion, Rashad was the most persuasive of all.

Deuce Scaife was a convenient, albeit very pleasurable, antidote to that. No one could be more different from Rashad than he was. When they met up that night, completely by accident after his traffic stop, she had taken her shot, partly to see what would happen if she did; and partly because he had— much to her surprise—been just as magnetic as all the rumors suggested.

Glancing at the face of her phone, she checked the time. He would be pulling up at any minute. And since she preferred to head him off at the front door, or better yet at the curb, she needed to get downstairs fast. The last thing she wanted was for her brother, Ousmane, to spot the car outside and suggest that she invite her guest in. His, and her father's more traditional sensibilities would be offended if she snuck out with some anonymous guy without at least introducing him for their inspection.

"Mia, let me catch up with you later," she said, cutting her friend off mid-sentence. "I need to get out of here before Ousmane starts getting on my nerves."

"Okay. But answer the brother's call, Zora. Even if you're not planning to get back with him, y'all can still do some good work together."

In that, Mia had a point. BLM was facing a lot of negative media backlash, and along with about a dozen other college chapters, there had been talk about having a stakeholder call over the holidays to strategize on how to counter all that. The problem with decentralized movements like BLM was that a few knuckleheads; or as was the case in New York, a lone gunman with misguided motives and a history of mental illness, could blow the whole thing up in one news cycle. Just because nationally, the movement lacked the resources to coordinate a rapid-response strategy.

They had lost a lot of ground over the past few months and were in danger of losing control of the media narrative altogether. But luckily, Rashad was a master strategist. If they had a stakeholder call, Zora was confident he would have more than a few good ideas for how they might recapture their hard-earned public support.

On the handful of occasions when he had been in the media locally, Rashad had owned the interview, coming across as articulate, thoughtful and commanding of the facts. His credibility had no doubt given credibility to the movement itself. Zora still remembered the hundreds of emails and text messages he had gotten from chapters and individual supporters around the country. The buzz online about him after one particular radio interview that past spring had enabled them to raise over ten thousand dollars for their chapter in less than a week.

In a word, Rashad Dixon was impressive.

"Admiration is *not* love, Zora," she whispered to herself.

It had become her own little secret mantra. Whenever she found herself faltering on her resolution to let her relationship with Rashad go, she repeated it. She could respect him, they could be friends and compatriots; but he was not, could not, and would not be more than that, ever again.

Taking a deep breath, she slung her bag over her shoulder and headed downstairs. Her timing turned out to be perfect. Just as she glanced out the window in the front room, Deuce's white Range Rover slowed and then stopped just in front of the house. Grappling for her phone, she shot off a quick text message to let him know she was on her way. And checking to make sure the coast was clear of her intrusive male family members, Zora slipped out of the house.

As she slid into the SUV, Zora turned to smile at Deuce, and he grinned back at her. Her stomach did a little flip of pure sexual excitement, even as her brain told her she was an idiot. It had been saying the same thing ever since she slid into that booth next to him at Beef & Billiards, but the rest of her body wasn't listening.

Mia and Sophie had been making eyes across the room with that friend of his, the track star with the Terrell Owens body and Lance Gross smile. And after a few minutes of that, he came over to invite them to join his table.

Zora knew of Deuce Scaife, of course, because his father was *the* Chris Scaife of recording industry fame; and his mother was notorious for her own reasons. From the time he was about sixteen, Chris Scaife, Jr. aka "Deuce" was the subject of blogger speculation. So, when word spread on campus freshman year that he had transferred from Notre Dame, everyone was curious, including Zora. But her curiosity had been abstract. She didn't care to meet him and definitely wasn't one of the groupies who started stalking his dorm almost from day one.

Besides, she had other distractions. Around that time, was when she met Rashad, one year ahead of her in school, and lightyears ahead in his political development. Whatever it was she saw in Rashad, he saw something with equal pull in her; and within weeks they were a unit. And so they had remained until recently. The Deuce Scaifes of the world may as well have existed on a different planet. But because the Black student body wasn't that large, word of his exploits sometimes made its way to Zora's ears.

And of course, she saw him around campus. Always with a different girl, but somehow the same type of girl. She was decidedly *not* his type of girl. No one could have been more surprised than Zora when, sitting next to him in Beef & Billiards and listening to his surprisingly arresting rumble of a voice, she felt her body angle itself toward him, her skin very sensitive, as though yearning for him to touch her. And that was part of why she went for it that night when he came to her room. He was to have been a curiosity and a diversion, nothing more.

But that only explained that one night. It didn't account for why she had orchestrated her way into a ride home with him from school, or why she had gone over to his house to watch a movie she'd seen many times before. Nor did it explain why she was here, with him right now.

"So why did I need to bring a swimsuit of all things?" she asked him as they pulled away from the curb in front of her house.

"Why does anyone ever need a swimsuit?"

He was wearing a long-sleeved white shirt that hugged the muscles of his arms and chest, and dark-wash jeans. Zora couldn't remember what position people said he used to play when he played football, but for sure he still had the body of an athlete. She could personally attest to its impeccable shape, even when relieved of clothes.

Blushing, she glanced out the window, worried that the memories of their night together might be visible on her face.

"We're going back to my father's house," he explained. "To swim."

"How do you know I can?"

"Can you?"

"Yes."

Deuce smirked. "You like being difficult, huh?"

"You shouldn't call people difficult," she returned, playing with the ends of her braids. "It's not nice."

"And if they are? What should I call them?"

"You should call them ... challenging."

"Yeah," he said slowly. His gaze met hers then he scanned her from head to toe in a way that made Zora feel as though his hands, rather than just his eyes were on her. "You're definitely that. *Challenging.*"

FOUR

She looked almost completely different.

When Zora had come running out to the car, she was wearing a knit hat, so Deuce didn't know, or think about what might be under it. He assumed her usual mass of hair. But when they got back to his father's place and she pulled it off, he saw that she had changed things up and now it was in eight neat cornrows, converging at the nape of her neck and fastened there in a shoulder length ponytail. With her hair no longer the focal point, it was easier to see her face, but now much more difficult not to stare.

She was standing at the edge of the pool, arms extended above her head in a pose that lengthened her already long torso. Zora had full, firm thighs, a small waist and an ass that looked to Deuce like it was sitting on a shelf. As for the breasts, he only wished he had taken more time to appreciate them that night back at school when he had a chance. But that night had been ... crazy. A frenzy of touching and tasting that left little time to examine, little time to truly savor anything other than the electricity between them. Even in the completely modest black swimsuit, her body seemed to be taunting him.

"This is the coolest thing ever," she said, lowering her arms again. "Swimming outside in the winter."

The steam rose off the water of the heated pool so he was viewing her through a partial haze. Standing in the shallow end, Deuce watched her set up and then execute her dive. She swam the length and surfaced, letting her head fall back as she did. The water streamed down her face then stood in silvery droplets on her skin, stark against its darkness. Deuce forced himself to look away.

"What was it like?" Zora asked suddenly. "Growing up with all this."

"I didn't really grow up in this house," he said. "I visited it. And not that often until the last few years."

"Why not?"

This was one of the things that most disarmed him about her—the way she asked questions, and made statements that most other people would have shied away from, her frank curiosity clear in her eyes. She had probably been the kind of precocious kid that her parents were always scolding: *Don't you know it's impolite to ask people that?*

Moving closer to him, using her hands to part the water, Zora stopped when she was only about six inches away. There was almost a foot in height difference between them, so she had to look up. When she did, her neck was exposed. Deuce remembered how he had kissed and sucked on it when he was inside her, and how she sighed when he did.

"I grew up with my mother. My father ... he wasn't around so much."

Zora's eyes were serious. She nodded, absorbing that information. "Was that difficult?"

Deuce cleared his throat, not sure how to answer her question. "It was what it was," he said finally.

Zora held his stare for a few moments more. "My Dad wasn't around much either," she confided, shrugging. "He traveled a lot between Senegal and the States. I think I was about fifteen before I realized that he and my Mom were basically separated. But divorce ... in our culture. It's just not that common, so I got used to him not being around and thought it was normal." She shrugged again. "But I guess it was different for you. Seeing your father on television and online but not seeing him that much in person. That had to have been tough."

Deuce said nothing, momentarily taken aback by how quickly and casually she sensed the *exact* thing that made the almost-estrangement from his father in his early years most difficult.

"Last night was a trip," she said, almost as if finally realizing she was treading on delicate ground. "Meeting K Smooth and his wife in your living room, like, just kicking back and drinking, I don't know. What was that? *Egg nog* or something, like regular folks."

"They *are* regular folks."

"I know. But you know what I mean. I swear when I walked into the room, even though there were maybe ten other people there, it was like there was a spotlight on him, he's so frickin' good-looking. Inhumanly so. I don't think I could handle a man like that. It would be too damn stressful." She laughed.

"You have one?"

"What? An inhumanly good-looking man? Ahm, *no*." She laughed again.

"Or even an average one."

Zora shook her head, but her eyes flitted away. Deuce remembered what Kal said about her and Rashad. Everyone knew Rashad. On campus, it wasn't even necessary to use his last name.

Zora leaned all the way back, and then pushed off to float away. That was a pretty slick bit of avoidance, but just as she was about to float away, Deuce held onto her left foot. Her toes were long and narrow, almost like fingers. The nails were painted a translucent pink. For a brief moment, he had the urge to kiss them. Instead he stroked her instep. Zora shrieked and yanked her foot away, abruptly standing, spluttering water.

"I'm ticklish!"

She was more than pretty when she laughed, she was beautiful.

"You hungry?" he asked. "I could have our housekeeper make us some burgers or something."

"Or ..." She let the word drag. "We could go out. This house is way too comfortable. If I hang out here any longer, you'll never get rid of me."

He nodded. "Okay, so let's go out."

He watched her get out of the pool, his eyes following the sway of her ass. Zora grabbed her towel off the chair where she'd placed it earlier and looked over her shoulder at him.

"You coming?"

The warmth of the pool, and the heated tiles surrounding it radiated only a few feet outward, so once Deuce told her where they were going, Zora dried her feet and made a mad dash toward the house through the icy cold and brittle grass, squealing the entire way. She waited for him at the threshold, the towel wrapped around her, and he took her hand, leading her down the long hall and toward the stairs leading to the second level.

Hesitating, Zora looked around. "Is this cool? I mean, your family ..."

"Yeah. C'mon." Without releasing her hand, he began his ascent and Zora followed.

On the landing, she tugged at his fingers until he stopped.

"Are you kidding me?" She paused in front of a series of paintings, lining the long hallway. "Are these *Kehinde Wiley*?"

Deuce shrugged.

Zora leaned in closer. "Oh shit. I don't think these are prints, either. These are ... *real*." She lifted a hand and slowly, moved it closer. Her fingers were almost trembling. Just before they made contact with the image, she pulled back and looked at him in amazement as though he was responsible for painting it himself.

"Robyn got them," he said, indicating the series along the wall. "She's the art lover in the family."

"Wow." Zora made her way slowly down the hall, her eyes still on the images, her hand warm and small in his. "It's been a long time since we had an artist like him. Whose work is so ... politically-relevant."

Her use of the word "we," Deuce knew, was meant to refer to Black folks. He didn't often think in those terms.

Finally pulling her hand from his, Zora made her way to the last painting, still clutching her towel around her.

"What makes it so political?" he asked. "I mean, they're really lifelike, but ..."

"And vivid, right? Hyperrealism is what it's called. The way he uses that to humanize Black people, especially Black men? That's part of what's political. Because Black men are most often *de*-humanized. This is almost like art as protest."

"Art is always protest," Deuce said. "Against conformity."

Zora's eyes opened just a little wider at that observation, but he was glad she didn't express her surprise verbally. And he was glad that when she explained Kehinde Wiley's work, she did it in a way that didn't judge him for not already knowing enough about something so unique that had been there, right under his nose and unnoticed.

Deuce turned to look at one of the paintings he had passed countless times without sparing it more than a few seconds' glance. The young man portrayed was holding his head up, his eyes almost insolent, his chin jutting forward. His neck was marked with a tattoo, and he was wearing a white undershirt and loose jeans. In his hand, he held something that looked like a staff, or a scepter.

"See?" Zora came to stand next to him staring at the painting; he felt her body heat radiating in his direction. "The way he stares at us? How defiant he looks? The ... majesty in his posture? How often do you see Black men depicted like that? Most often, they're slouching, frowning. Angry. This makes them look like nobility. Like ..."

"Kings," Deuce said.

Zora turned and looked at him instead, nodding, her face solemn. "Yeah," she said, her voice barely above a whisper. "Like kings."

Taking a step closer, Deuce saw her inhale—her shoulders lifted, and as she released her breath, they fell. Her skin was like polished mahogany. Deuce smoothed his thumb across one shoulder, watching Zora's eyelids droop, ever so slightly. He could see in them that she was feeling some of what he felt.

"Are we going to eat, or what?" She sounded like she could be talked out of that plan. But the house was overrun with family, so getting out was probably a good idea.

"Yeah," he said. "Let's go eat."

ON THE TABLE BETWEEN THEM, Zora's phone buzzed.

It was facedown, so she reached for it, grimacing when she saw who was trying to reach her.

"Excuse me," she mumbled, sliding out of her seat.

Deuce watched her walk over to an alcove near the entrance to The Cheesecake Factory where they were having lunch. Around them, there were still traces of Christmas cheer, the booths and walls decorated with red garlands and poinsettias. Zora's head was down as she talked to the person on the phone. She raised a hand to her forehead, then to the back of her neck, balancing her weight on one foot and then the other. Whomever it was, was making her either uncomfortable or irritated. He couldn't make out her face, so he couldn't decide which.

It was a dude. He could tell by her posture.

Reaching for his own phone, seeking a distraction, Deuce dialed the number of one of his friends who lived not too far away. Patrick McKenna was a tall, redheaded kid who, like Deuce, was a child of privilege. They knew each other from the expensive football camps they had both attended in their early teens, and because Pat had a stable of friends that had nary another White boy in sight.

He was the kid that, when they were growing up, you wanted to pull to the side and say, '*Dude, you* do *know you're not Black, right?*' But Pat, or "Paddy" as Deuce once heard his father call him, was cool people, and when Deuce was in Short Hills, he could always be counted on to know where the parties were.

"You're in luck, my man," Pat said. "Tonight, the only place you'll wanna be is Casa McKenna."

"Word?" Deuce asked. "Where's the fam at?"

"In Aspen. Or Vail. The fuck if I know. But they ain't here, that's the important thing."

Pat's family was, like Deuce's, blended. His father had

married a woman who looked basically like a newer model of Pat's mother, and who had recently had a new baby. And Pat's mother, too, had moved on to her second family. Because of that, Pat, as the remnants of a failed marriage neither parent wanted to be reminded of, was frequently casting about on his own during holidays. So, on second thought, that was nothing like Deuce's family, because if it had come to that, he knew his stepmother would have driven herself up to Penn State to get him rather than let him spend a holiday alone.

"So what time you tellin' folks to come through?"

Across the room, Zora had wound up her phone call and was heading back his way.

"Anytime you want, man. It's an all-day and all-night bacchanal over here."

"Cool. I'ma check you out later then."

He hung up, just as Zora slid back into her seat, signs of strain on her face.

"You good?" he asked.

If he had to guess, he would say the person she had been talking to was definitely Rashad. He could see it on her face, feel the weight of him on her spirit. Because Rashad would be heavy, the kind of dude who would occupy every inch of his woman, or at least try to.

"Yup. Good. Sorry about that. It was a call I had to ..." She reached for one of her sweet potato fries and popped it into her mouth, chewing at it desultorily.

"You sure you a'ight?"

She looked up at him, her eyes suddenly intent.

"You know when people have this image in their head of you?" she asked. "And you feel like you're always doing battle with that image? Fighting to live up to it, or ... live it down?"

Deuce nodded slowly. "Yeah."

A glimmer of realization lit Zora's eyes. "Duh. Of course you do." And then after a pause. "Well, it sucks."

"What're you trying to live up to? Or live down?"

She shrugged and reached for another fry. "Just ... stuff."

"I have an idea," Deuce said, grabbing one of the fries off her plate.

"Yeah?"

"Why don't we just ... shed all that? Both of us. Until we go back to school, we just let all that go, and enjoy this time. Enjoy ... each other."

"By that you mean ..."

"You know what I mean," Deuce said.

Zora looked down at the table, tracing a pattern with her finger. Finally, she lifted her eyes to his again, but still, she said nothing.

"You know how hard I've been tryin' not to touch you?" he admitted. "It's wearing me out."

Zora smiled. "Then don't try anymore," she said.

By the time they got to Pat's house, the party was in full-swing even though the sun had only just gone down. Deuce held Zora's hand as they entered, because the foyer was crowded and the music so loud, the only way he could communicate with her was through touch. There was dancing in the living room and on the enclosed porch, but the press of bodies was so thick, it was more like a mosh-pit. Deuce and Zora were pressed together, and jostled back and forth. After a few moments of that, Zora threw her hands up in defeat and started bouncing to the beat.

Deuce laughed and bounced with her, both of them losing themselves in Drake's raspy and rough voice. There, on the dance floor, they let go of everything that was weighing them down and became just a guy and his girl, dancing.

Around midnight, Pat invited a few people upstairs to his

room where it was quieter, and they lay around on the rug, passing a spliff and watching music videos. When the weed made its way around to Zora, she took it and inhaled a long, deep toke, held the smoke in for a long time, and then released it. Her eyes were bleary and unfocused. She looked at Deuce looking at her and gave a half-shrug.

"Karaoke!" Pat announced out of nowhere. "*That's* what the fuck we need!"

The two girls flanking him whooped their approval of the plan.

"Lemme go find my shit," Pat said, stumbling to his feet, and heading out of the room. Deuce's eyes followed his friend then came to rest on Zora again. She was smiling, the vaguely hazy smile of someone who is as high-as-a-kite, and maybe even a little drunk too.

Standing, Deuce went over to her and extended a hand, pulling her up. With a hand on her waist, he moved her closer, so their chests were pressed together. Her breasts were soft against him, her breath was a little smoky, a little boozy, a little sweet. He was a little high, too. High enough to hold her as though preparing for a waltz, and swaying, a little too slowly for the rapid beat of the music coming from Pat's oversized television.

Pressing his lips against her ear, Deuce spoke. "Still having a hard time not touching you."

"You *are* touching me," Zora said, her mouth against his neck.

He shivered a little. It had to be the weed, the music ... something else. It couldn't just be her.

"Nah," he said. "I want to touch you ... more."

Zora pulled back a little and looked him directly in the eyes, motioning toward the door.

Holding hands, they shoved their way downstairs and

Deuce looked wildly around, trying to recall where in Pat's house they might go to be alone. He tried the library, the powder room just off the kitchen and even the pool house. Everywhere they checked, someone else had gotten there before them. Feeling increasingly desperate, he tugged Zora along behind him until she yanked on his arm, pulling him down to her.

"Where's your car keys?" she asked.

Deuce looked at her inquiringly. "The car?" he cupped his hand at her ear. "But we're probably blocked in."

"So we'll stay there ... in the car," she said.

"For real?"

Zora nodded, her eyes holding his.

It was almost pitch-black outside, save for the dull, yellow glow of the streetlights and the path-lighting leading out of Pat's father's house. Together Deuce and Zora made their way past the dozens of other cars and halfway down the street to where they parked hours earlier. With Zora shivering next to him, Deuce fumbled with his keys before his chilled fingers found the fob and finally managed to unlock the doors.

Zora reached past him and yanked open the rear passenger-side door.

"Get in," she said, her voice urgent.

In the near distance, the music was still loud. Deuce thought for half a second about the neighbors. The houses weren't too close together, but it was only a matter of time before someone thought to call the police to break things up, or to get Pat to at least tone them down. And if they rolled up and some car was all fogged-up and rocking, having the party come to a premature end would be the least of Deuce's worries. So whatever was about to happen right now would have to happen quick.

Climbing in ahead of Zora, he slid over to make room for

her, but she didn't need it. As soon as he was in, she clambered in after, and on top of him, slamming the door behind her. Cupping his jaw, Zora kissed him, her tongue sliding immediately past his lips. Deuce grabbed her hips and ass, pulling her closer. Zora's hands dropped from his face and she fumbled with her bra then grabbed his hands, sliding them under her shirt and over her breasts.

Her nipples hardened under the touch of his still cool hands, and she moaned into his mouth, their tongues unrelenting. His hands moved down to her waist and he lifted her shirt. Zora leaned forward and Deuce bowed to instead capture a nipple in his mouth, tugging at it with his lips and feeling the pliant, almost rubbery texture against his tongue. She smelled clean, and a little like the chlorinated water they'd been swimming in earlier in the day. If he could, he would have swallowed her whole, she tasted so damn good.

"Oh ... oh god," Zora gripped his shoulders. "I need ... right now. I need ..."

Deuce reached for her skirt, dragging it upward bunching it into his fists without removing his lips from her skin. Raising herself up, her knees on either side of his hips, Zora grappled with the fly of his jeans.

"Wait." Deuce lifted his head.

Zora froze. "*What?*"

Lifting his butt off the seat and reaching into his back pocket, Deuce slid out his wallet, and tossed it onto the seat beside him. "Condom," he said. "Should be a couple in there."

"Okay, so get one." Zora lifted herself almost completely up, and began the painstaking process of removing her panties. And when she had, and Deuce saw it—a frilly white thing—his dick jumped and twitched. He couldn't get to the damn condom fast enough, and his jeans and boxers seemed to be conspiring against him. Zora batted his clumsy hands aside and released him.

For a few seconds, she looked down, studying his size and girth. Her chest heaved as Deuce worked on ripping the condom packet open with his teeth.

"*Shit!*" he said. He'd ripped not only the packet, but the condom itself. Tossing it aside, he reached for his wallet again while Zora giggled.

"Ain't nothin' funny about this," he said. "There better be ..."

Finding another one, he opened the packet, this time with much more care, and then sheathed himself. By then, both he and Zora were practically panting. Holding her hips, and simultaneously holding her skirt out of the way, Deuce guided her down onto him. He wanted to watch her face, he really, *really* did. But against his will, his eyes rolled back, and his head fell back against the seat. The car was almost cold inside, but Zora was all heat.

Clasping his arms tight around her, Deuce held her close against him, soaking in the sensation. The scent and feel of her transported him almost immediately back to that night in her dorm room. It *wasn't* just a trick of memory, it was just as good as he remembered. Better. He let his hands drift downward, and Zora's ass filled his hands.

She arched her back with the barest of motions and at the same time clenched her thighs tighter. Deuce opened his eyes and looked up at her. She was staring down at him, her eyes dazed and fixed, her lips slightly parted. Deuce bowed his head, lifting her shirt with one hand, running the tip of his tongue around one nipple and then the other. As he did, he felt Zora squeeze him tighter, heard her make an almost agonized sound at the back of her throat.

"Zee," he groaned. "Damn ..."

"I know," she said. "I know ..."

He *felt* her coming, even before she cried out and her fingers dug into his shoulders. Wanting to see her face, Deuce opened his eyes again and looked up just in time to see her grimace and throw her head back. A shard of moonlight entered the car and illuminated her long, slender and exposed throat.

Her dark skin was, in that moment, golden.

DEUCE'S FRIEND, Pat, was giving a terrible rendition of The Delfonics' *'Didn't I Blow Your Mind?'* and the two girls who had been hanging on him all evening were attempting to sing back-up. Zora laughed, stretching her legs out in front of her, reclining between Deuce's widespread knees and against his chest. Maybe it was the weed, or more likely the interlude in his car, but she felt comfortable there. She even felt comfortable in the bedroom of this guy she didn't know from a can of paint, listening to him sing karaoke to songs she would never have imagined he knew about in the first place.

Occasionally, Deuce shifted and she thought she felt his semi-turgid dick against her butt. And because he kept shifting, she was inclined to believe that that was precisely what it was. She couldn't even believe she had done it—just screwed him in his car outside of a party.

It wasn't the kind of thing she did, habitually. Rashad took complete charge of their sex-life, and would have balked at anything that risqué. He was hyper-attentive to this idea he had in his head that she should never be treated with anything other than complete respect. It was a value Zora appreciated, but sometimes it didn't leave room for spontaneity of the type she'd indulged in tonight with Deuce.

And why the hell was she thinking of Rashad now, anyway? They were done, and she was having fun. She was ... what was that phrase Deuce used? She was shedding expectations. Just for now. In a week and a half, they would be back in school and Zora would resume the strictures imposed on her by her position on campus. But for now, this was good.

Deuce was laughing as Pat messed up a high-note, and Zora felt his chest rumbling against her back as he did.

"You think you can do better, nigga?"

She tensed, waiting for Deuce's reaction to his unmistakably non-Black friend calling him by a name that was reserved only for those of the darker hue. But there was none. Instead, he only laughed louder.

"Put on some Teddy P," he said. "I'll sing the hell outta some Teddy Pendergrass."

"Who?" one of the other girls asked, wrinkling her brow. She was a blonde, almost painfully skinny but undeniably very pretty, who had been giving Deuce the eye all night. She didn't do it directly, but with her peripheral vision, occasionally using her hair-toss as an excuse to turn her head in his direction. Her interest in Deuce made Zora feel possessive, not just on her own behalf, but on behalf of all Black women. But Deuce's hands, even now on her shoulders and her waist, and sliding along the length of her thighs couldn't seem to stay still. So Zora knew that despite what happened back in his car, he still wanted her. If she was reading his body correctly, there was nothing further from his mind than the skinny blonde chick giving him the eye.

Black girl magic, bitch, she thought smugly.

And then she felt badly for thinking anything like that, because the poor girl couldn't help it if Deuce was fine as hell, could she? Damn, she had to be drunk. Because why else would she be looking to start a race war up in this boy's house?

"Here's some Teddy P for yo' ass," Pat said, cuing some-thing up on the karaoke machine. His face was florid and sweaty from all the drinking he'd been doing, his eyes bloodshot from all the weed he smoked.

Zora moved so that Deuce could get up and take control of the mic. Clearing his throat, he looked at the monitor.

"Yeah," he said. "This is my shit right here ..."

The strains that signaled the start of Teddy Pendergrass' 'You're My Latest, My Greatest Inspiration' began. Prepared to be amused, Zora leaned back on her extended arms smiling as she watched Deuce circle his neck as though loosening up for a title boxing match. Pat came and collapsed on the floor next to her, and Deuce began to sing.

Almost immediately, the smile melted from her face.

Deuce had a rich and deep speaking voice, but his singing ... Zora would have been floored, if she wasn't already sitting on one. He was *good*. Even Pat, who had been poised to ridicule him seemed to be struck silent.

"Oh. My. *God*," one of the other girls said.

But Zora was too riveted to take her eyes off Deuce who similarly, seemed not to be able to take his eyes off her. Zora's stomach tightened, and when he got to the lyrics '*And I'm thankful, yes, I'm blessed just to know you ...*' she thought she might pass out.

"Goddamn," Pat whispered next to her. "This shit is rigged."

One of the girls laughed. "You can't *rig* karaoke!"

"He's from a musical family!" Pat protested.

Everyone held their breath when he got to the end of the song and hit that last note. And damned if he didn't pull it off. Zora stared, feeling the start of a tiny pulse between her legs.

When the music faded to silence, Deuce tore his gaze from

Zora's and looked instead at Pat. Holding up the mic, he opened his fingers and let it drop.

"How ya like me now?" he asked, his face deathly serious. "*Nigga.*"

Zora's eyes widened. Hearing the steely irony in his voice, she realized that what she'd assumed earlier could not have been further from the truth. Deuce *did* notice Pat's use of the word. And he hadn't liked it any more than she had.

By the time Deuce felt he was sobered up enough to drive, it was after three in the morning and Zora knew there was no way she would be able to go rolling up to her house and stumbling in with marijuana-face. So instead she texted her brother and told him she was crashing with one of her high school friends, and that he should smooth things over with their parents. For himself, Deuce had to text his mother, and then together, they headed back to his father's house.

They didn't speak for the first few minutes after they settled on that solution. As he drove, heavy in the air was the knowledge that she and Deuce would be for-real '*spending the night together.*' Zora felt her heart beating in her chest as fast and hard as though they hadn't already turned each other out a few times now.

"That was fun," she said, her voice hoarse with nerves.

"Yeah. Pat's always good for that."

"And y'know what?" She turned in her seat as much as the seatbelt allowed. "You can like, really sing. I mean, no kidding around ..."

"Thank you," he said easily.

"Seriously," Zora said, hand on his thigh. "I mean, you can *sing.*"

He glanced over at her. "*Thank* you," he said again.

She shook her head. "You think I'm just saying it because you didn't completely butcher Teddy P."

"No, I hear you," he said. "I just don't ... care about performing."

Zora nodded, watching him.

In profile, he was even more handsome. The lines and sureness of his jaw were emphasized, as was the strong, solid column of his neck. He was clean-shaven, so looking at him straight-on, he was almost pretty. But from this vantage point, she could see the man he was, and the man he would become. He would only grow better-looking with age. His nose had a high and narrow ridge, and his lips were full and sensual while still masculine. It was difficult to look at them without wanting to kiss him.

"So, you're not going to be looking for a record deal with your father's company, huh?" she teased.

"Nope," he said, his tone a little short.

The car fell silent again and Zora touched his thigh. Deuce looked at her, and shrugged.

"The entertainment business," he began. "It's not ... it's not what people think it's like. All that stuff you see on TV, that's not even ... It's different than you think."

"Okay, so what's it really like?"

"Lots of fake shit," Deuce said, almost scornfully. "It brings out the worst in some people."

"No plans to work in the family business then?"

He looked at her. "I didn't say all that."

"So, you will work in the fake-ass entertainment business after all?" she asked laughing.

"Never mind. You wouldn't understand."

"No. Tell me." She touched his arm.

"There's the music entertainment business and then there's the music business. They don't have to be the same. They're not always."

"Okay ..."

"The way the entertainment business is set up, they intertwine a lot. Sometimes too much," Deuce explained. "So, the music part of it gets lost. Overshadowed. And the real artists sometimes get overshadowed as well."

Turning a little in her seat so she could keep her eyes on him, Zora nodded, prompting him to continue.

"So yeah, I'd want to work in my father's company but what I'd want to do is curate. Y'know what I mean? Find the artists who're advancing the art, not just selling a lot of records. I mean, something like that would probably mean a loss, maybe even a big loss at least at first, but the trick would be to gain a following. Small to begin with, but ..."

"Wait. Something like *what*?"

He was talking faster, because it was obviously a subject that excited him, something he cared about.

"A label. A small, specialty label, that looks for the real deal. Not just the folks we can package and sell because they have good hair and a passable voice."

Zora smiled at the phrase "good hair."

"That sounds amazing," she said truthfully.

Deuce glanced away from the road and at her. "Yeah, but the part where it would take a loss? That's the tricky part. I'd have to sell that one real hard to my father. He doesn't like to lose. At anything."

Shrugging, Zora reached out and touched his arm again. "But the good news is that he's your father. So you have to have some inside knowledge about what he would find persuasive."

"Hard work. That's it. He respects hard work. He came up with and from nothing, and made a multi-million-dollar company. All he respects is blood, sweat and tears."

"Then I guess you'll have to find a way to demonstrate some of that."

Deuce looked at her again, and Zora shrugged again. "Right?"

"Yeah," he said. "Right."

"So ..." she said after a few moments. "How do you plan to sneak me into your room?"

Turned out, sneaking wasn't necessary. The large house was as quiet as a tomb when they pulled through the front gates and up to the front door. But once Deuce shut off the engine and got out of the SUV, motion-sensing lights activated nearby.

"Shit," he mumbled. "Forgot about those."

Holding her hand, he led her along the side of the house, toward the back and through another entrance. Moments later, they were treading quietly and carefully up the wide and imposing staircase. Once they were in his room—if it could be called that—at the end of the hall, Deuce shut the door and leaned against it. Then he tugged Zora toward him, and looped an arm around her waist.

"I want you again," he breathed against the shell of her ear, the tip of his nose brushing her skin.

Turning her head, Zora answered by sweeping her lips across his. "Then have me."

FIVE

Zora removed her shoes and put her bare feet up on the dashboard, humming along to the low and mournful strains of Joni Mitchell. The heated seats in Deuce's SUV made her eyelids and limbs heavy, and her thoughts sluggish. She was still tired, having gotten very little sleep the night before. *His fault.* She glanced at Deuce out of the corner of her eye and wondered whether she should have declined the invitation to drive with him to Bedford, New York where his mother lived.

She's pissed, Deuce confided. *Said I haven't spent enough time at home this Break.*

And when Zora told him that probably wasn't the time to bring some girl along, he insisted that his mother wouldn't care that much; that she just needed to know he was close by, and then would basically leave them to do their own thing.

Zora still shouldn't have agreed to come. But she was getting used to it now—the routine where she kept telling herself not to spend this much time with Deuce and then being unable to follow through.

"How much longer?"

"Just enjoy the ride, Zee. We're almost there."

"You said that like thirty minutes ago."

"I'm drivin' slow, that's all. It's not that much farther."

"Why *are* you driving so slow?"

"You never heard of black ice? And take your smelly-ass feet off my dashboard."

"You *kissed* these smelly feet night before last," she reminded him in a sing-song voice. "I think you even *sucked* these smelly-ass toes."

"I was drunk," he said. "*Really* drunk."

Zora laughed and nudged him in the arm. "You were not. You were completely coherent. You told me I tasted like honey ... and that you ..."

"Yeah, yeah. Shut up."

Zora looked at him, and he was looking back at her, biting his lower lip to smother a grin.

"You always this silly?" he asked.

Zora shook her head. "No. Actually, I'm never this silly," she said truthfully. "Only with you for some reason."

"That's right. You and your crew walk around campus like Black Panthers ... all serious like this ..." Deuce mimicked a scowl.

Zora tried to smile, but she didn't want to think about campus, and she didn't want to think about her "crew."

She could only imagine what they would all think of her being with someone like Deuce, even casually, even temporarily.

"Prepare me for your mother," she said sitting up. "What's she like? How did she and your Dad meet?"

She let her feet drop to the floor and Deuce reached over, placing a hand on her thigh, high on her leg. So close ... and yet so far.

"She can be tough sometimes," he said. His hand on her leg

was moving back and forth, stealing toward her inner thigh, and then away again. "But she's pretty cool."

"And how'd she and your father meet?"

At that question, Deuce gave her one of the looks he sometimes gave her, where she could tell he was wondering whether he should answer, or be more guarded about family details. It was probably one of the hazards of having a famous parent.

"Sorry. That sounds like I'm prying. I always like to hear those stories ... love stories. I guess because my parents met through an arranged marriage."

"For real?" Deuce sounded skeptical.

"Yup." Zora nodded. "Not like her parents sold her for a hundred cows kind of thing, but yeah, it was arranged."

"How'd that happen?"

"My mom grew up in Chicago. She was NOI..."

"NOI?"

"Nation of Islam."

"Oh. Right."

"And then when she came to New York for college, she learned more about mainstream Islam, and became a Sunni and started going to a local mosque. After she'd been there a while, the imam approached her, and told her about a young man he met, who he said he thought would be a good husband for her. A devout man, who was walking the right path."

"And so just like that, she married him?"

"No. She said she wasn't into it at first because after all, she's still a modern American girl, right? And then she said one night she had a dream where someone was talking to her. She said she didn't even remember what he said, but the voice stuck with her because it was so ... stirring, so compelling."

"Okay ..."

"And then three weeks later, when she had just about

forgotten the dream, she was eating in a restaurant with a girl-friend and the waiter came over to take their order. She said when he said good evening, she immediately recognized it as the voice from her dream. So she became curious about him, asked his name, and talked to him a little while they were there in the restaurant. Turned out he was Muslim too. And worshipped at the same mosque as her.

"They agreed to stay in touch. Just to keep talking. And a few days after that, she found out he was the young man the imam spoke to her about. The young man he said should be her husband. So my mom decided that there were too many signs, too many coincidences, and that Allah had put this man in her path, to be her husband. And a month later, they got married." Zora shrugged when she was done.

"You're making that up," Deuce said.

"Nope. Totally true story."

"Well I hate to disappoint you, but my parents don't have anything like that. Theirs is about as far from a love story as you can get," he added.

"They don't get along?"

Deuce made a scoffing sound. "Yeah, you could say that."

"My parents' story isn't much of a love story either," Zora said, shaking her head. "They've been separated for years, pretty much. My father's from Senegal, very conservative, wanted a submissive wife, had all these ideas about marriage that my mother, I don't think could buy into. They kind of live together, I guess ... they share the same house and bed when my father's in the country. But they're separate. They don't under-stand each other, and they've basically stopped trying." She shrugged again. "But anyway, that's why I like hearing love stories about other people's parents. The opposite of everything I saw at home when I was growing up."

"Did they fight a lot?"

"Not at all, actually. My father would never raise his voice at my mom. Would never disrespect her. He's a devout man, just like that imam said. But the distance ... I think that's just as painful, probably. My parents, they're both ... they seem so ... lonely when they're together."

Deuce squeezed her leg and Zora realized she probably sounded sad, so she looked at him and forced a smile.

"Do you think your mom was wrong?" he asked.

"What d'you mean?"

"You said she thought God was putting signs in her way, that this was the man who was meant to be her husband. So now, do you think all that was wrong?"

Zora thought for a moment. "I think there are no signs. Not from Allah, not from anywhere. You just should do what makes the most sense for the life you want. Always. And that's probably what she should have done."

DEUCE'S BEDFORD, NY home was just as impressive as the New Jersey one. Though considerably smaller, its façade was like that of an English boarding school; red brick, with symmetrical rows of windows—eight on both sides—and an imposing front door with a brass knocker. The casual way that Deuce shoved his key into that door, and nudged it open with his hip told Zora how comfortable he was in surroundings that most average people would find intimidating.

Her parents had made a nice home for her and her brother, a nice life. But nothing like this. The foyer was grand, and everything in it arranged as though for showing a model home. There was not a single item within view to indicate that people lived there—not a pile of mail, nor snow boots at the entrance, nor a coat closet, half-open and bulging with winter wear.

"Ma!"

When Deuce yelled out, somewhere in the house, there was the sound of someone approaching. Moments later, there was his mother, standing at the top of the staircase. For a second, Zora narrowed her eyes. Because his mother was beautiful, and looked like no one's mother. Slender with long, pin-straight dark hair, parted in the center, she had a face that was one of contrasts—an almost angelic rosebud of a mouth, combined with a shrewd and narrow face, and dark, piercing, suspicious eyes.

But most interesting was the fact that the woman seemed to be completely, and professionally made-up. Though dressed in a baby-blue tracksuit, suitable for lounging around at home, her makeup made her look like a cast member on a reality show.

And it was that thought, which made Zora suddenly begin to remember, piece by piece, all the little tidbits of information she had heard about Deuce Scaife's mother. Much of it was unpleasant. Some of it downright scandalous.

"Took you long enough," she said as she descended the stairs.

When she was finally standing in front of Deuce, it was clear how petite she was; no more than five-three, and probably light as a feather. But Zora was intimidated nevertheless.

"So you don' live here no more?" she asked, twisting her lips and looking up at her son.

She hadn't acknowledged Zora at all.

"Just hangin' out with old friends in Jersey," Deuce said, leaning in to kiss her on the cheek. "That's all."

"'Cause you have no friends around here?" His mother rolled her eyes.

"Anyway, Ma. This is Zora." Deuce angled his body toward

her, and Zora felt visible once again. "We drove up from school together."

Deuce's mother let her eyes drift toward Zora and travel from head-to-toe, then up to her head again, lingering on her Buckwheat hairdo. After what seemed like an eternity, she lifted a small hand and extended it.

"Hello. I'm Sheryl."

"Nice to meet you, Miss Sher..."

"No. Just Sheryl. I ain't hardly old enough for nobody to be tacking Miss in front of my name. Y'all hungry, go ahead get Gayle to make you something." She dropped Zora's proffered hand, then turned to head back upstairs. But thinking of one last thing, she paused again to look at Deuce. "And don't be runnin' off back to Jersey without lettin' me know neither."

"You hungry?" Deuce asked turning to look at Zora when they were alone again.

She smirked at him. "Why? Because you'll have *Gayle* make me something?" she teased.

Shifting his weight Deuce's eyes avoided hers. "Yeah. The housekeeper."

"I am hungry," Zora said. "But let's not trouble *Gayle*. Why don't you give me the house tour and then we can go eat someplace else? Like maybe somewhere you used to go when you were a kid. I want to get the full Deuce Scaife Lifestyles of the Rich and Famous treatment."

"This how it's gon' be?" he asked, looking amused. "You messin' with me about how I grew up?"

"Nope. Not at all. Show me everything. And introduce me to all the servants."

Zora followed Deuce through his home, which was no less a showpiece in the other rooms than it was in the foyer. But there were occasional signs that it was occupied by someone who liked things ostentatious—gilded and sometimes gaudy embellishments to a house that did not need it, and lots of labels, even on the crockery displayed in a massive cabinet in the dining room.

After seeing all the rooms downstairs, Deuce took her to his large bedroom on the second level. It was decorated with football memorabilia, trophies, and posters. Even the comforter represented his favorite team, which was apparently the Baltimore Ravens. This room, unlike the one at his father's house, was more like that of a teenage boy. Piecing together everything Deuce told her, Zora assumed this was the room he left behind when he went to college; the room that had been his high school room.

Zora sat on the bed and looked up at Deuce, who was also looking at her, a hard-to-read smile on his face.

"What's funny?" she asked.

"Seeing you here. Sitting on my bed."

"Don't get any naughty ideas," Zora warned. "This house isn't nearly as large as your father's place."

"Nah." He sat next to her, very close. Close enough that she could feel him though they didn't touch, and smell the light scent of his cologne. Or was that just soap? Either way, he smelled really good, and Zora was the one getting 'naughty ideas'. "I was just thinking how a month ago, I never would've thought you would be here. Of all people."

Zora lifted her eyebrows. "We didn't even really know each other a month ago," she said.

"But I knew who you were," Deuce said, his eyes fixed on hers, searching them.

Tiny hairs stood up on Zora's arms.

"And what did you think of me?" she couldn't help but ask.

He shrugged. "I don't know. I didn't. But if I *had* thought of you, I'd probably never imagine you as the girl who'd be here. Sitting on my bed. What'd you think of me?" Then he gave a brief laugh. "Oh yeah. I forgot. You told me what you thought of me on the drive up here."

Zora blushed, remembering her words and how harsh they sounded. They were kinds of things you said to someone when you had judged them from afar with limited, and probably faulty information. It embarrassed her now.

She shook her head. "I didn't know you. Those were just ... I'm sorry I ever said all that stuff. It was ... obnoxious."

Deuce leaned in, brushing his lips lightly against hers. "I forgive you." He spoke against her lips then pressed in closer, sliding his tongue in and tasting hers.

Zora held very still, letting him lead the kiss. He was patient, slow, and sensual in the truest meaning of the word— he used his lips and tongue to explore her, always taking his time as though seeking out the most perfect, and sweetest spot of taste and texture. No one had ever kissed her with that much care before.

Sometimes when they kissed, she grew dizzy and disoriented with it. Once, in his room in Jersey, when they were going at it, making out like high-schoolers, she lost awareness of anything except Deuce's mouth on hers. The room, the time of day, the sounds of his father's busy house had all disappeared from her consciousness, so that when she next opened her eyes, she was surprised to find herself on her back, still fully-clothed, but legs open and Deuce between them.

Now, he held her lower lip between his, sucking lightly on it and then with the tip of his tongue, enticing hers once again. Zora moaned into his mouth and heard how anguished it sounded, beseeching and begging him for more. He gave it to her, with his hands in her hair, grabbing and gripping it, holding her to him, and answering her sounds with low throaty groans of his own.

When he pulled back, that was slowly as well. They

parted, but he nudged her nose with his, and his warm breath swept across her mouth. Zora felt a slight tingle in her lips, the nerve endings screaming for contact once again. Deuce's forehead was touching hers, and he exhaled again.

"*Damn*, Zee," he breathed.

SIX

Two nights before he met Zora, Deuce had been dodging phone calls and drop-ins from a senior named Caroline Farber. Caroline was a lean blonde who used to be on the women's track-and-field team, but saw her track career end with a bad ankle injury. She still hung out with the athletes and went to their parties though, which was how Deuce met her, two weeks before he found himself in the position of trying to avoid her at all costs.

Standing at the edge of the room, alone with a red Dixie cup she'd been sipping from all night, she looked comparatively cool when almost all the other girls were in that drunk-and-sloppy time-zone that came somewhere around two a.m. Deuce had looked her over, appreciating her long legs, and the way her skin was so tan, contrasting with her almost white-blonde hair. She wore it in a loose top-knot, like she just wanted it out of her way.

Don't mess with her, Kal warned, when he noticed him looking. *That's girlfriend material.*

Deuce scoffed at that, because he didn't do girlfriends. But he didn't heed the warning and after talking Caroline up for an hour, he asked her back to his room.

I don't just go home with random guys, she said.

She said it three times before she did just that. And in his room, she tried to extract meaningless promises while he undressed her: *Promise you don't think I'm a total slut? Promise you don't think less of me?*

When he woke up the next morning, she was gone and Deuce was relieved because if they were there when he woke up, he always felt obligated to walk them back to their dorm. And since it was twenty degrees outside, he wasn't in the mood.

By the time he showered and got dressed for the day, Caroline's face was a vague memory. Until he saw her downstairs. She had been waiting for him, she said. After she went back to her apartment to get showered and changed, she thought he might want to spend the day together.

Spend *the day* together. That sounded to him like an interminable length of time.

He told her he had some work to catch up on and she seemed to take it in stride, but asked him if she could call later, and maybe when he was done ...?

And for the next thirteen days, Caroline Farber called him at least twice a day and stopped by his dorm at least once. Each time she left messages that sounded and seemed perfectly casual. Except that there were so many.

I told you not to mess with her, Kal said.

You said she was girlfriend material, Deuce said. *I thought you meant she was the kind of girl I might want as a girlfriend.*

No, nigga. I meant she's the kind of girl who needs to believe she could be your girlfriend before she'll fuck you.

Zora Diallo was not that kind of girl.

After their unplanned interlude, when he woke up in her room, in the early morning hours, she was just getting done folding a shirt and tossed it into her suitcase. Her room, which earlier had been a mass of laundry and papers, and bags strewn about, was clean.

Slept okay? she asked. Her voice was soft, almost tender.

He nodded and grinned at her. He couldn't help smiling, because she was standing there in a long, baggy t-shirt, and her messy hair was even messier still. And her bare legs were just long, and dark, and smooth, and ... incredible.

Good, she said. *It's almost dawn. I'm leaving today.*

The timing—her departure from school the morning after a one-night stand—should have been ideal. After all, he had just been through all that mess with Caroline. But he wasn't relieved, and didn't want her gone so soon. He wanted to talk to her some more, touch her ... give her reason to make those sounds she made when he was inside her.

You sure you have to go? he asked.

That's the plan. But it doesn't mean we can't, you know ...

She pulled the sheets away from him, and stepped forward, at the same time lifting the shirt over her head.

Then she was on top of him. He rose partly to his knees, and she cupped his head, wrapping her arms around his neck.

Your tongue, Deuce remembered her saying. *I want to feel it ... give me your tongue.*

Give me your tongue. It sounded strange, like she wanted him to cut it out and present it to her as a gift. But in that moment, he almost would have. Cut a part of himself off from the rest, and given it to her.

Whatever part of him gave her pleasure, he wanted her to have.

ZORA WAS LAUGHING with her whole body—head and

shoulders tossed backward, a hand at the base of her throat, gripping it as if to hold in her uncontrollable mirth.

So fucking cute.

Choking as she swallowed a mouthful of pizza, she finally caught her breath and reached for her cup of soda, taking a long, deep gulp.

"Now that's funny," she said when she could finally speak.

Deuce looked on as his friend Clarence leaned in for another slice of pizza. He had been giving Zora the rundown of all the dumb stuff they had done together when they were in high school—smoking reefer behind the gym, breaking into the girls' locker room and showers ... the usual stupid high-jinks kids with too many resources and no sense of purpose did. When Clarence first started talking, Deuce inwardly cringed, thinking how it all must sound to Zora, who had probably been organizing protest marches when she was six.

But instead she listened to every story, nodding in encouragement, rapt, and then amused and then curious. Her explosive laughter had been a response to Clarence recounting how they'd hosted a full barbecue and skinny-dipping party after hours on a weekday at their high school's Olympic-sized pool, and been caught by school security.

"Cops were called ... the whole damn thing was a cluster," Clarence concluded, shaking his head. "The girls were freaked out ... the guys were naked. And man, when there's a cop staring you down, the shrinkage is real."

Zora spluttered into laughter again. "I bet." And then, across the table she exchanged a look with Deuce.

Somehow, he knew she was thinking about his most recent encounter with the police. And more than that, she was probably thinking what he was thinking—that Clarence, who could pass for one of the Kennedys, had a little less reason to be apprehensive about a run-in with law enforcement. Back then, at an exclusive prep school, caught trespassing, Deuce had no fear. But now he realized that was probably because he had a bunch of guys who looked like Clarence with him.

"You guys hanging out?" Clarence asked. "We could head into the city, hit up some clubs ..."

"I don't know," Zora said. "I think I might make it a quiet one tonight. But I'm sure this guy will be into it." She winked at Deuce as she stood and excused herself to go to the ladies' room.

Clarence watched her leave and leaned back in his chair, eyebrows raised. "So, what's her deal?"

"What d'you mean?"

"I mean, you know ..."

"Yeah," Deuce said, meeting Clarence's gaze head on. "That's me."

Clarence's green eyes met his, and his friend smirked, but his brows furrowed in confusion. "How'd you even meet her?"

"I told you; school. And I don't know if you've heard but there's like ... twenty-five Black people at Penn State so we pretty much all know each other."

Laughing, Clarence shook his head. "Yeah, okay."

"Okay, that's an exaggeration, but just barely."

"I'm jus' sayin,' man, you have to admit, you weren't exactly one to seek out 'the brothas'," Clarence said, making quotes with his fingers. "Or 'the sistahs' either. No matter how few of them there were."

"The fuck?"

"All I'm saying is, she's definitely not the chick I would expect to see you with. With the hair, the whole look, man ... she's just ... different for you."

"Y'know what? Just shut the ..."

"Deuce, I was more likely to date a chick like Zora than you were. Admit it. I mean, it's not a big deal. We all have our tastes, and mine always ran *way* darker than yours. That's all I'm sayin'."

Deuce looked at Clarence, whom he had known since he was about four years old and suddenly in that moment, he had never seemed Whiter.

By the time Zora returned, the silence was tense.

"We're going to roll out," Deuce said, looking around for the waiter. "Good seeing you, man."

Zora looked confused at the abrupt change of mood but said nothing, just watching him as he settled the tab, her eyes fixed on his face as though trying to read it. When he'd paid, Deuce stood and gave Clarence a cursory nod, leading Zora out to the car.

He opened the door and waited for her to get in then walked around to the driver's side, taking deep breaths to control his persistent irritation. But it didn't work, because when he got in, Zora shot him an inquisitive look.

"What happened in there?" she asked.

"Nothing. Why?"

"Because I came back, and you both were staring daggers at each other. When I left, you were the best of friends, and then …"

"Clarence and I were never 'the best of friends'. I've just known him for a long time."

"And so what ha..."

"Have you ever dated White guys?"

Zora shook her head and laughed. "Whoa. Whiplash! What brought that on?"

"Forget it," Deuce mumbled.

He started the engine and backed out of the parking space, pulling out into the light traffic. Christmas was just a few days behind them, so the streets were still quiet, as people rested and recuperated from the frenzy of spending, celebrating, and overeating.

He'd only been driving for a couple of minutes when Zora reached across the distance and rested her hand on his leg.

"No, I never dated White guys," she said. "And it wasn't for want of them trying. I just never ... I don't know." She shrugged. "I wasn't interested enough in anyone, or curious enough to say yes when someone stepped to me. Why?"

"Just wondering."

"Did Clarence say something?"

Deuce looked at her. "He was interested. I told him you weren't available to him in that way."

Then Zora's hand was at the back of his neck instead, and she was giggling. "Aw, did that make you mad?" she teased. "That he wanted to take his shot?"

"Nah. It just made me wonder."

"About my dating history with the Clarences of the world? So here's the deal. I guess I could have dated White guys, but part of me always worried that I would never know whether for them dating a Black girl, especially a girl as black as me ... was the point. Y'know what I mean?"

Deuce glanced at her and shook his head.

"I mean, I didn't want to be anyone's social experiment," Zora said baldly. "I worried that I would never trust them enough to believe I wasn't just that. Didn't you ever wonder that? With the girls you dated?"

He shook his head again. "No."

"See that's the difference between us. I've always had a high degree of race consciousness. I mean, it defines so much of me. And you ... where you grew up, how you grew up ..."

"Don't try to fit me into one of your little theories, Zora. I know I'm Black. I've always had that awareness. Just because I don't form Black Lives Matter chapters or march every time some kid gets dropped ..."

Her hand fell from the back of his neck. "Fine. Since you brought it up ... No one said you needed to be an all-out activist, Deuce. But to live as though you're oblivious to the struggle of people who look like you? *That* I don't get."

"Why am I oblivious? Because I don't protest every single injustice on the planet?"

"Not every single one. The ones that pertain to people of color. That's what we're talking about."

He let out a puff of breath. "Y'know what? Let's just drop this shit."

"No, let's not," Zora said firmly. "Because unless I'm mistaken, you just got all in your feelings when your friend in there wanted to make a move on me. But god forbid Black women should have something to say about all those little White girls *you* run around with. I mean, if we ever dared to ..."

"Race has nothing to do with it!" he snapped.

Zora gave a bitter laugh. "It never does, does it? Especially not for guys like you ... who seem to have a distinct preference for women of races *other* than your own. Never mind that you were the one who asked if I dated White guys. So for you to say that ..."

Swinging out of the lane and to the side of the road, the two passenger-side tires mounting the curb, Deuce brought the car to a halt and put it in park.

"I wouldn't give a shit if he was *green*, I wouldn't want him crackin' on you. You understand that?"

Zora looked stunned for a second and then her lips twitched. She shook her head. "Except there *are* no green people," she said slowly, "so ..."

Exhaling in exasperation, Deuce reached for the gearshift, but Zora's hand covered his. Her thumb moved across his knuckles, and then she turned his hand palm up, lacing her fingers through his.

"Hey," she said, her voice low.

Deuce looked at her, and she gave him a little smile, leaning in to kiss him lightly on the lips and then letting her forehead rest on his shoulder for a moment.

"What I said before? That was really condescending. I'm sorry." She sat upright and looked directly at him. "I mean it. I'm really sorry I said that thing about your ... low degree of race consciousness, or whatever. That was untrue and ... and ... uncalled for."

"It's not untrue though," Deuce said. He leaned his head back against the headrest. "At least, not completely untrue."

The car fell silent. Zora was waiting for him to go on.

"I've never not been *aware* of being Black," Deuce said. "But in my life, it just ... the significance of that isn't the same as it is for most brothers, y'know what I mean?"

"No," Zora said quietly. She put her hand atop his again, a silent encouragement for him to go on.

"I grew up in a life that was almost a, I don't know, I guess you could call it a defiance of the stereotypes that other Black men have to live with. So, I didn't grow up in poverty, but with money; not being shut out of exclusive places, but being invited into them; not feeling like there were some girls who were off-limits, but knowing I could have any one I wanted."

Deuce heard the gentle intake of Zora's breath, as though she had just realized or been made to understand something she never got before.

"But being the Black *exception*," Deuce continued. "The one who supposedly defies the stereotypes? I'm not sure that's any more fun than being the brother who lives up to them."

"It is though," Zora interrupted. Her tone was gently challenging. "You have to see that. The consequences for a regular Black dude for things *you* get away with ..."

"But what do I get away with though, Zee? Going to nice clubs, dating girls people get uncomfortable to see me with? The bottom-line is, when it gets down to the most basic stuff, the life-and-death shit? Like getting stopped by a cop and not knowing how its gon' go? Me and the brother who didn't have my privileges, we're *exactly* the same."

"Deuce, you're not," Zora said, shaking her head. "You have access to recourse, you have ... visibility ... assets a lot of people don't have. So, what you do with all that? It *matters*."

"How'd we wind up talking about race politics anyway?" he asked, shaking his head.

"Dude. Seriously? Do you know who I am?" she teased.

Turning to look at her, Deuce stared, his eyes locking with hers. Reaching out, he touched her hair, taking it between his fingers and feeling its unyielding strength. "No," he said, tugging on it. "Who *are* you?"

HE COULDN'T SLEEP. He was tired, but couldn't bring his mind to the restful state his body was crying out for. Deuce went to stand on the terrace in the bracing cold, wearing only a t-shirt and boxers. From this vantage point, he could see into the dark and almost to the edges of his father's property. There were lights that bounded it, dim and concealed in the trees, twinkling like distant promises.

Some of what he'd said to Zora that night, he hadn't even known he was feeling—that it was tough living his life as an exception? Where had that even come from?

Objectively speaking, his life wasn't tough. Not by a long-shot. But there were times, when he did things he didn't necessarily want to do so much as he wanted to prove he could: '*I can do this, have this, be here ... and yeah, I can even fuck her. Even though I'm a young, Black man. And even if you don't like it.*'

Or maybe he was rationalizing; transforming into a form of rebellion what was just plain old bad behavior and entitlement. He didn't even know for sure which was true; because these were questions he never would have asked himself, but for meeting and spending all this time with Zora Diallo.

When he told her he didn't care what Clarence's race was, just that he was interested in her, that wasn't true. At least not completely. He wouldn't have liked it if anyone had tried to make a move on her even if it was another Black dude. But there was no denying he liked it even less, because Clarence was not a Black dude. And that realization was messing his *whole* game up. Because what did it mean about him, and his choices?

He was shivering now. The temperature had just morphed into something else altogether, and now was bitter. Turning to head inside to his bed, Deuce decided that before a brother could spend time thinking about whether he was about to be woke, he'd have to work on getting some sleep.

SEVEN

"I just don't think it's constructive, Michelle. What's the point in being so inflammatory?"

"What the cops did is what's inflammatory. All we're doing is holding up a mirror to it."

Closing her eyes and trying to summon calm, Zora sat on the edge of the sofa and counted to ten in her head. Michelle was the manager of the BLM chapter website, and was given wide berth to decide on content. Most days she posted information about rallies and networking events, links to new publications from watchdog organizations like the Southern Poverty Law Center, and to recent civil rights data. Zora had never tried to micro-manage her choices, even though she could as co-chair of the chapter.

But this morning, checking in on the website as she customarily did, she saw that Michelle had posted a graphic montage of police shootings, beginning with the one of Oscar Grant, handcuffed and sitting on the ground in the BART station on that fateful and horrible day. The video was jarring, and had been presented without any context—just a five-minute excessive force horror reel.

"Look, I texted Rashad before calling you back," Michelle added. "And he was cool with it, so ..."

Zora held the phone away from her ear and mimicked a scream.

"Well then let me call him directly. We need to sort this out, so please pick up if I call you again."

"I don't know if I can promise that. I'm out shopping with my sister and them for New Year's Eve outfits so if I don't hear the call ..."

"Okay, fine. Well, just check your phone in about an hour. I'll leave a message if I don't get you."

"Zora, I did my time working on the website today. So, if you want something pulled, I'm sorry, you just might have to do it yourself."

Oh, no she didn't.

"You're our site manager," Zora said sweetly. "If that's a job you no longer want, please let me know."

On the other end of the line, Michelle made a snorting noise. "Just call me when you know what you want to do about the video. I gotta go."

When the connection broke, Zora screamed aloud, and tossing her phone across the bed, threw herself down next to it. She would need a moment before calling Rashad. After all, she had been avoiding his calls most of Winter Break, and he would no doubt want to get into that as well.

"What's the matter with *you?*"

Her brother Ousmane stuck his head into her room, no doubt hearing the blood-curdling noise she'd just made. Zora lifted her head but didn't bother sitting up.

"Just some stuff to do with the BLM site."

Ousmane shrugged. "I'm sure you'll handle it."

Her brother was a senior at U. Penn., a chemistry major and very much a head-in-the-clouds scientist. He was proud of her social justice work, but viewed it from afar. He related much more closely to their Senegalese roots than Zora did, and like their father, considered American race issues with more academic interest than emotional connection.

"Actually, I'm going to need Rashad to handle it," Zora said with annoyance. "Because the chick who does our website apparently needs to hear something from a *man* who's in charge before she feels moved to act."

Ousmane lifted his eyebrows.

"Of course, you think that's perfectly fine."

"I didn't say anything!" Her brother laughed. "How's Rashad anyway?"

Rashad and her brother had met a few times when Zora went to Philadelphia to visit him at Penn. And each time, her brother and boyfriend had talked past each other, though both came away thinking the conversation had gone perfectly fine.

"Okay, I guess. I haven't spoken to him that much since I've been home."

"Oh. So ..."

"Yes," Zora said, before he had a chance to ask the question. "So."

She and her brother traded stares for a few beats then Ousmane smiled at her and tapped on the doorframe.

"Well carry on then," he said before ducking out again.

Taking a deep breath, Zora picked up her phone and called Rashad. It rang three times before he answered, sounding a little out of breath.

"Did I catch you at a bad time?" she asked.

"Any time's a good time when it's you."

Despite herself, Zora smiled. If there were such a thing as

heartstrings, Rashad sure knew how to pull hers. And that was part of the problem.

"Ahm." The confrontational tone she'd planned to take seemed no longer relevant. "I just talked to Michelle. About the video on the website? She said you told her it was fine to leave it up there?"

"Look, of course I don't like the footage. Of *course* the images aren't easy to stomach. But we can't whitewash this shit, Zora. Police brutality is ugly. And it doesn't stop just because it's the Christmas holiday."

"But it's not new news, Shad. Michelle was just being lazy and went for shock-value instead of searching for new content. And besides, we're not looking to pointlessly inflame people. We're looking to motivate them."

"And some people are motivated by anger."

"Yes, but it has to be directed anger. Coherent anger. Not just *blind* anger. The video doesn't even include a call to action, nothing to add to the conversation we're trying to start."

There was a brief silence and then the sound of Rashad's laughter. "Damn, girl. *This* is why I love your ass, you know that? I don't know too many people who're takin' time out of their holiday cheer to worry about shit like this."

"Rashad. Call Michelle and tell her to take it down. She doesn't listen to me. She needs to hear the word directly from you."

"Okay. Consider it done."

"Thank you," she said, exhaling.

More silence.

"I'm headed back to school a little early. There's that piece the guy from the local paper wanted to do on us. Could be some positive media. And there's a couple other things we could take care of, like prepping for the all-chapters conference call. You wan' ride with me?"

"The local media is a little hard to pass up," she admitted. "So yeah. I'll see whether I can make it back a couple days before classes. But the dorms won't be open, so I don't know where I'd stay."

"C'mon, Zora. With me, at my apartment. I can be honorable. Sleep on the couch and all that. And maybe we can talk too, y'know?"

"Rashad."

"What? We broke up. That means we can't talk anymore? That's one of the things I miss most about us. How we talked. Like no other couple in the history of mankind. Epic-ass conversations about life, and love and ... politics ..." Rashad broke off and made a sound like breath whistling through his teeth. "Everything. Just ... those conversations we had were *everything*."

Zora closed her eyes, squeezed them shut as tightly as she could.

"Rashad."

"Anyway, lemme let you go. You caught me between sets at the gym. I'll call Michelle as soon as I get done here and tell her to take down the video."

"Cool. Thanks."

"Anytime, baby."

Baby. Why did he have to go and call her baby?

Just hearing the word, spoken from his lips and she could picture him, stroking his long goatee as he spoke. She used to grab ahold of it when they were in bed together, and stroke it while he moaned with pleasure.

Damn baby, I love it when you do that, he'd said to her once.

Zora wished she could forget how much pleasure she derived from his pleasure. Rashad was the first man in her life. In high school, there had been boyfriends, of course. And dates. But none were with guys she thought of as full-grown men.

Rashad, even though just twenty-one was so completely who he was, so sure of his values and opinions. And even when she met him two years ago, he always felt far ahead of everyone else, accelerated somehow. So much so that he'd accelerated Zora as well. Just to catch up, she had to push herself in ways she never would have without him.

Without him, she wasn't sure she would take her life and the world around her as seriously as she now did. Without him, she probably would have been flailing around like some of her friends, still trying to figure out who they were and what they believed in.

"Hey. Before you go. What you up to for New Year's Eve?"

"A party," she said vaguely. "You?"

"Watch Night Service with my mother and grandmother," Rashad said. "Maybe I'll check out a couple spots with some friends after."

"Pray first, sin later?" Zora teased.

He laughed. "Yeah. Something like that. But since you won't be with me, I don't see too much of a certain kind of sinning in my immediate future."

"*Shad*," Zora said. "C'mon. Stop."

"Yeah, I know," he said. "But feelings don't turn off that quick, Zora. You still have my heart."

Closing her eyes, Zora wiped a hand across her forehead. *This was why.* This was why it was better not to talk to him at all.

"Anyway, I'll let you go," he said again when after almost a minute, she still hadn't responded. "Enjoy your New Year's Eve, Zora. We'll talk on the other side."

"You too, Shad."

Shad. He told her she was the only one who had ever called him that. And so, she'd clung to it, feeling good that she had a piece of him that no one else had.

Zora hung up and had put her phone down for no longer than two minutes before a text message came through. Expecting it to be a last-minute thought from Rashad, she smiled when she saw that instead it was Deuce.

What you wearing for me tonight?

What do you want me to wear? She typed out her answer, still smiling.

Nothing, came the response. *I want you to wear nothing at all.*

Yeah. Okay.

And since sarcasm didn't translate in text messages, her phone rang right away.

"You serious?" he asked. "You want to go somewhere?"

Zora laughed. "How do you propose to skip your father's New Year's party without someone noticing?"

"He has over two hundred people coming. He's not going to be thinkin' 'bout me."

"You're his son. I think he'll notice if you're missing," Zora insisted.

"Maybe." Deuce sighed. "So, what're you really wearing?"

"A dress."

"Yeah?" he prompted. "So ... tell me about it."

Zora looked at the phone for a second and smiled again, shaking her head. He meant it, too. He *wanted* to hear about her New Year's Eve dress.

At first, she thought for sure this trait had to be part of his technique—active listening to make girls think he gave a crap about what they were saying, drawing them in with displays of false interest. But he had already drawn her in.

Just about every time they saw each other, they wound up in some quiet corner, pawing each other, his hands down her jeans, under her shirt, his mouth on her neck or behind her ear. And once, with his entire extended family only about a hundred yards away in the great room, he'd pulled her into the coat-room and backed her up against the wall, crouching, lifting her leg over his shoulder and giving her the best head she had ever received in her young life. *In the coat-room.* As though he couldn't even withstand the amount of time it would take to get her upstairs.

Wait, Zora had whispered, her heart pounding with the fear of being discovered. *Wait, Deuce. Later. We can … later.*

No, he whispered back, his voice urgent. *Not later. Now.*

And then with his mouth and tongue, his hands gripping her thighs hard, he made her come in forty seconds flat. The sex, the laughter, the fun, the recklessness of being with someone who was clearly wrong for her. If only it wasn't so damned … addictive.

"It's white," she said now, of the dress she planned to wear.

"Long, or short?"

"Short."

"Good," he said. "That's good. Easy access."

Zora laughed. "Shut up. Have me actin' like a complete 'ho."

"Just can't get enough of you, that's all."

Zora swallowed. If that was just a line, he sure as hell delivered it convincingly.

"So …" She cleared her throat. "I have to get home around five a.m. or so. I need to spend *some* time with my family this Break."

"We got a whole week after."

"Well. No. Not really. At least, *I* don't have a week. I'm thinking of heading back a little early."

"Why? What's up?"

"BLM business," Zora said, trying to sound casual.

"How you getting there?" Deuce asked. "I could …"

"You don't have to do that," Zora said short-circuiting the

offer. "I ... I'll get another ride. Because, you know, it's earlier than ... earlier than planned."

Smooth, Zora. Very smooth.

The silence on Deuce's end lengthened.

"How're you getting there?" he asked again. This time he was more than curious, he was almost ... demanding.

"I'll get a ride," she said again.

The unasked question hung there like a gray storm-cloud above both their heads.

"I'll swing by 'round eight to get you tonight," Deuce said. He sounded different.

"Yup. I'll be ready." Zora tried to resurrect the lighthearted tone from earlier in their conversation. "Carrying my short, *short* white dress."

Deuce laughed, but it sounded false. "Alright," he said. "Rest up. It'll be a long night. And don't forget to bring something to wear for brunch tomorrow too."

"Yes sir."

"WAS THAT WEIRD?" Zora asked.

She was in Deuce's room at his father's house, lounging around in front of his large-screen television, half their attention on a movie they had both seen before, and the rest on each other. They hadn't said much, but Deuce's head was in her lap, and Zora was idly raking her fingernails across his scalp while his eyes grew heavy.

It was almost nine-thirty, and downstairs, the house was aflutter. Caterers were bustling back and forth, the first guests were arriving and the loud pulse of music could be heard from the open terrace as the revelry got underway. They planned to get dressed and head down around ten, when things would be in full swing.

"Was what weird?"

"The way my father and brother grilled you."

When Deuce came to get her, the usual routine of her running outside to meet him at the car hadn't worked. This time her brother was lying in wait, and the minute she grabbed her things, he'd clamped a hand on her shoulder and said he thought it would be better if he invited her "friend" inside.

Zora knew better than to refuse. So Deuce came in, and for forty excruciating minutes, Zora watched her father and brother take his measure. Her mother had ducked in to say hello, but didn't participate in the third-degree. She was the only one in the family who wasn't in denial about the fact that Zora wasn't exactly living the life of a good, Muslim girl. Hell, she even ate pepperoni on her pizza.

"Nah. I mean, we've been hanging out a lot, right? And sometimes I bring you home like around three in the morning. I get that they'd want to know who this dude is who doesn't even come up to the front door."

"I just want to make sure you know it doesn't ... mean anything," Zora stuttered. "Just like I've met your parents, it's not like I've 'met your parents', y'know what I mean?" She made air-quotes with her fingers.

On her lap, Deuce's eyes suddenly became alert. He sat up and shifted so he could look her in the eye.

"What d'you mean?"

"I mean ..." She cleared her throat. "It's just the circumstances, right? But soon we'll be back at school, and ..."

"And?" Deuce prompted. His dark eyes had grown darker still and his brow was furrowed.

Zora wasn't even sure what she was about to say, but something told her it was certain to be the wrong thing. Then, thankfully, there was a quick series of knocks on the door and Deuce's step-mom stuck her head in.

She was a very pretty woman, with a girlish air about her, like someone who loved their life and just about everyone in it. And why wouldn't she? Because even though she had a full house of guests, and a baby on her hip pretty much constantly, she also had a husband and extended family who obviously adored her.

Tonight, she was wearing an emerald green sateen dress with demure cap sleeves a square neckline, and short bell-skirt. Accessorized in gold, she looked luminous. This was a woman who clearly knew what colors accentuated her honey-toned complexion.

"You two look way too comfortable for a couple about to go to a party," Robyn said. "C'mon and get ready." She clapped her hands as she spoke, to denote urgency. "We want the entire family downstairs."

Deuce was still looking at Zora like he had something to say, but she was relieved for this chance not to hear it, and quickly stood.

"I still need to take a shower, so half an hour?" She glanced at Deuce and he nodded, though slowly as if his mind was elsewhere.

"What are you wearing?" Robyn looped an arm through hers as they walked together down the hallway in the direction of the guest suite where Zora had been installed.

"A white mini-dress. Something I recycle every once in a while, for big occasions like these."

"Sometimes you have to go for those old favorites," Robyn agreed. "The ones that make you feel beautiful no matter what. This dress is five years old." Then she put a finger up to her lips and made a *shh* sound.

"I won't breathe a word," Zora laughed.

"Okay. See you downstairs, love. And please, don't let Deuce get in front of that television again. He's just like his father ... never met a party he didn't want to get out of."

Zora smiled politely, not wanting to burst Robyn Scaife's bubble. Deuce's rep was *exactly* the opposite. But hell, everyone had an alter ego that they presented to the family.

And not just the family either, Zora thought as she shut the door behind her. To friends as well. The Zora Diallo who would be returning to school in a few days didn't feel like the same girl as this one, who was giddy and silly every single day just at the prospect of spending time with a guy whose deepest preoccupation wasn't the state of the world, or race, or politics, but just ... her.

EIGHT

"She's pretty chill, huh?"

Deuce turned to look at his friend, Stevie who had draped an arm over his shoulder and was leaning on him a little heavily. Stevie was one of a handful of friends from Bedford who he had invited to his father's New Year's Eve parties for years now, since the days when he had to sneak a couple of drinks, instead of walking around openly with a glass of amber-colored liquid like he was doing now.

Standing on the edge of the dance floor, he watched Zora dance with Kaden. With each clownish move his little brother made, Zora laughed and mimicked it, which only made Kaden amp up his antics. Now, he was doing a strange twitching move, crossing his hands on his knees and flinging his head back and forth. Zora studied him for a few moments then did the same.

On the other side of the dance floor, Deuce saw Robyn watching them as well. She caught his eye and smiled, giving a small shrug. Feeling his face warm, Deuce wondered whether he was that transparent.

"Yeah," Deuce said, turning his attention to Stevie. "She's pretty chill."

On the dance floor, Zora was making flapping motions with her arms, following Kaden's lead. With each upward motion, the hem of her dress lifted, exposing more of her long, dark, shapely legs. On her feet were delicate, silver high-heeled sandals. Even her toes were sexy.

The music changed to something slower and Zora smiled down at Kaden, using her hand as a fan and making an 'o' with her lips as if to say, '*phew, that was hard work!*' Kaden grinned back up at her, his eyes filled with the kind of adoration that you can only get away with displaying openly when you're not yet ten-years old and in the throes of your first crush. Deuce wished he had that luxury, because the way he wanted Zora, the way he *craved* her made every other time he'd wanted a girl seem false, and dim by comparison.

Striding out among the swaying couples, Deuce put a hand at Zora's waist. She spun to see who had made the contact and her face opened into a wider smile.

"Scat," Deuce said to Kaden, before pulling Zora closer.

Putting both her arms up and about his neck, she shook her head. "Scat?" she said.

"He's taking up my time."

"It's only eleven thirty-nine," Zora pointed out, glancing over to where a large digital clock had been set up above the deejay's station. "You've got a whole twenty-one minutes left to spend with me in 2015."

"What're we doin', Zora?"

Deuce felt her tense in his arms.

"We're shedding expectations," she said eventually, her voice tense. "Enjoying each other. Aren't you? Enjoying me?"

Deuce closed his eyes. "Don't *say* shit like that," he said, holding her closer.

"Why?"

"You know why."

"I don't know," she said. "And I don't know what we're doing, either."

"How're you getting back to school?"

"I told you." She tensed once again, confirming what he had already guessed at.

"Why you leavin' early?"

"Deuce. I told you that too."

"BLM business," he said. "With your co-chair?"

At the nape of his neck, Zora was lightly raking her nails back and forth. She was trying to soothe him, the way she did when they were falling asleep together and he fought it, because he wanted more of her. Always more.

Since that night after Pat's party, there had been three others when they managed to spend the entire night together. She fell asleep in his arms and he awoke the next morning, opening his eyes and studying her. The curves of her face, the slope of her hips, the length of her legs, the linear, manicured patch of hair between her legs.

Once, Deuce had even pulled back the sheets and traced every detail of her body with his eyes—the obsidian circles of her areolae, the impenetrable dark-brownness of her skin, her smooth, flat stomach, full thighs and lush ass; and back up to her face, staring at her long, curled-at-the-ends eyelashes and vaguely puckered lips. And then before she even came fully awake, he had grabbed a condom and putting it on, moved above her, parting her knees with one of his and sinking between them.

Your libido is out of control, she murmured sleepily before opening up to welcome him in.

"Yes," she said. "With my co-chair."

Deuce wrinkled his nose and sniffed. It was a habit he had

when he was angry and had no outlet to express it. But why should he be angry now? This was what they had signed up for, both of them—something that would pass the time over Winter Break, a diversion until they returned to their real lives and the expectations that came along with that.

Despite all this—whatever *this* was—she was still Zora Diallo, campus revolutionary and young-woman-on-the-move, and he was still the resident aimless, rich kid.

"*Fifteen minutes, folks!*" The deejay's voice interrupted the music. "If there's someone you love, someone you'd like to welcome 2016 with, I'd suggest you find them right now."

There was a flurry of activity on the outskirts of the dance floor as people scurried around to follow those instructions, but Deuce didn't move. He was precisely where he wanted to be.

"It's almost 2016," Zora said, smiling up at him.

"Yeah," he said. "It is."

Though the music sped up, they remained wrapped around each other, for one song, two, and then the third. And when the countdown began, Deuce leaned in to kiss her. They were still kissing, still in each other's' arms when the ball dropped and the room erupted in cheers.

ZORA WAS asleep when Deuce staggered out of the bedroom Robyn had put her in. It was down the hall from his own suite, where he was supposed to have slept after the festivities were over. He was halfway there when he collided with his father, making his way upstairs.

Glancing over Deuce's shoulder toward Zora's nearby room and then down the hall to Deuce's, he narrowed his eyes, opened his mouth to say something, then stopped.

Relieved, Deuce nodded a wordless acknowledgement and continued toward his room.

"*Deuce.*"

He stopped at the sound of his father's voice. Turning, he waited.

"You being careful?"

Giving a barely perceptible nod, he averted his eyes and continued down the hall. The truth was, last night, after the first two dances of 2016, Deuce and Zora had escaped to her room. And there, for the very first time ever, they *hadn't* been careful.

Standing in front of him, Zora had raised her arms, at the same time lifting her wisp of a dress over her head and letting it fall at her feet.

You said you wanted me in nothing for the New Year? she asked. *Well, here's your chance.*

They were both a little drunk—Zora on champagne, and Deuce on all the drinks he'd been knocking back most of the night trying to take his mind off her impending early departure, and who she would be departing with.

Advancing toward her, Deuce had unfastened her bra and peeled her underwear over her hips, crouching as he did. There, on his knees in front of her, he shoved her thighs apart and tasted her, energetically lapping until she grabbed his head, pressing herself against his mouth. He couldn't seem to get enough of her, ever. But more so last night. He didn't stop until she issued a deep groan, that wracked her entire body, and her legs buckled.

He loved going down on Zora. *Loved it.* The way she tasted, the way she felt and most of all the feeling that he had complete control of her in those few minutes. And the control was important, especially with this girl for whom he was beginning to have feelings that were uncontrollable.

He and Kal joked about it all the time—their infantile scoring system for how much a girl had spun them out. *Man,* they might say. *I* even *ate the yum-yum.* Because if a girl made you want to do all that, she was definitely something.

With Zora, it was an every-single-time deal. Because she deserved it, and he wanted it.

Holding her up, Deuce stood, and pushing her back onto the bed, he stripped down to nothing. Zora watched him as he did, with rapt attention, the rise and fall of her chest visible. Once between her legs, he didn't enter her right away. Instead they kissed, grinding, and sliding back and forth against each other. She tasted so good, and her lips were so soft that for a long time, Deuce lost himself in just the kissing. And when, purely on instinct, he lifted his hips and slid effortlessly into her, unsheathed, it was too late to turn back.

Zora clutched his ass, her fingers biting into him. She groaned and spread wider, hooking her legs around his to anchor herself, and to give him the leverage he needed to push even deeper. Lips still locked on hers, Deuce pressed himself against Zora, as though he wanted to disappear inside her. And why not? Because he was already long gone, and long ago lost.

Even when he felt his approaching climax, the idea of pulling out, and pulling away hadn't even occurred to him. In that moment, Deuce couldn't have done so even if someone had flung the door wide open and invited the entire party inside to witness their coupling.

So, no. He hadn't been careful. But he couldn't make himself regret a second of it either.

ACROSS THE TABLE, Zora was yawning hugely. Lifting a hand to cover her mouth, she smiled apologetically.

"I'm sorry," she said to the general company. "I think I probably need a few more hours' sleep."

Robyn laughed. "I can appreciate that. I think I could use a few more myself. After you get something to eat, feel free to crash until you're in fighting form again."

"Thank you," Zora said graciously. "I appreciate the offer, and it's been so much fun. But I really should get home to see my family."

Deuce looked up from his plate, and tried to catch Zora's gaze but she was moving her eggs around.

For some inexplicable reason, as soon as he saw her that morning at brunch, he was pissed. He was already downstairs on the patio eating with Robyn, her brother, Nate, and her mom, when Zora came to join them, wearing pink velour sweatpants and a long-sleeved white tee with bright-white tennis shoes. Her hair, which the night before had been wild and free, she had pulled back into an Afro puff. With no makeup and no jewelry, she was a little swollen around the eyes.

She smiled at Deuce and said 'good morning' to everyone before walking the length of the buffet table and choosing eggs and lox for her plate. Touching Deuce lightly on the back of his neck as she passed him, she chose a seat opposite his at the table and began reviewing the party with Robyn and her mom, complimenting the food, and the decorations, and sharing how excited she had been to see some of her favorite musicians.

She didn't really give much of a crap about seeing famous musicians, Deuce knew. But if she had seen Anderson Cooper, or Van Jones, *then* she might have been excited. She was being polite, and making conversation, but behind her smiles, and her studious pretense of interest when anyone else spoke, Deuce could see that she was already thinking about what she had to do next.

What she had to do next was go home, spend time with her family and plan her early departure back to school with Rashad.

Rashad Dixon had been there with them for the entire week and a half they had been hanging out. Just offstage, an unacknowledged and heavy presence that Deuce sometimes sensed at unexpected moments. He showed up most often when they were laughing, or clowning around. Like when they'd gone to a dive bar where Deuce tried to teach her how to play pool and Zora had accidentally catapulted one of the balls across the room, almost beaning a waiter right between the eyes. They had both doubled over in laughter, while the waiter stood there looking none too amused, his eyes wide in shock at his near-miss with a concussion.

Looping his arms around Zora's waist, Deuce kissed the back of her neck and pried the pool cue from between her fingers.

Lemme take that, he said, turning her around in his arms. *This ain't your game.*

And for a moment she smiled at him, nodding her agreement until just as quickly, the smile disappeared and he saw in her eyes the exact second when some unspoken memory replaced it.

There were other moments like that—like the afternoon they spent in his room playing video games on his Wii, both of them only partly-dressed. After hours of aimless gaming, they napped on and off, and had lazy, quiet, furtive sex, excited and frightened at the possibility that someone might just wander in on them, opening Deuce's unlockable door. Later they went down to the kitchen and scavenged a meal, then returned to nap some more.

When Deuce opened his eyes again, the light outside was a gray and dim, wintry dusk; he and Zora had slept most of the day away. Or he had anyway, because Zora was awake and leaning on one elbow, looking out toward the French doors leading out to his terrace.

Do you realize, she said. *That we just spent like ten hours doing nothing at all except satisfying our basest desires? It feels so ... wrong.*

Jesus, Zee, what're you talking about now? He had moaned, turning over onto his stomach and dragging her against him.

Later he would remember what she'd said and think of how the words sounded as she spoke them. Like they weren't her own. Like she was channeling someone else's ideas—someone who would make her feel guilty that even though she was barely twenty and a college student, she had spent one afternoon eating, lazing around and having sex with her boyfriend.

Except he wasn't her boyfriend, Deuce thought now as he glanced over at her again.

He was her Winter Break.

He was a "base desire" that she felt badly about indulging in.

NINE

"Human relationships are complicated," Rashad said. "You can't rig that shit. It just happens the way it happens."

Zora said nothing, keeping her hands folded on her lap, listening to him talk.

Usually, she loved listening to Shad talk. He had such agency of expression, such complete command of his words. They were currency for him—buying him entrée into circles where most young, Black men would never go. After Penn State, he was going to law school at Stanford, and after that, who knew? The sky was certainly the limit for someone like Shad but he wanted to be out West. He liked that he was going to be close to Oakland, because like lots of East Coast Black activists, he was in love with the city as the birthplace of the Black Panther Movement and imagined that there, some of the magic from that time would rub off.

"And I definitely understand why you were curious about him. I mean, hell, how many like him we got out there, apart from the ballers?"

He was talking about Deuce. Because after an hour of

barely-disguised curiosity about how inaccessible she had been to him over most of the Break, he guessed that she had what he called "a fling" with someone. So, not wanting to act like Deuce was a dirty secret, and most of all wanting to put an end to the probing, Zora had just come out with it.

I drove home with Deuce Scaife, she said. *And we wound up spending some time together over Break.*

Yes, they spent time together. Lots of time. And then there was New Year's Eve which was amazing. Scarily so. So scary that when Deuce had taken her home the next morning, Zora ignored all his calls and texts, instead immersing herself in her parents and brother for the next day and a half, then packing all her stuff to return to school.

She called Shad late on the night of the third of January, and suggested that they get going sooner rather than later. He was there before nine a.m. on the fourth and they had hit the road in his reliable but beat-up Toyota 4Runner.

Today, she knew for sure, Deuce would give up calling and stop by her parents' house. He would have exhausted his limited patience by now; and knowing her planned departure date would simply show up. He was spoiled in that way. Spoiled in *every* way, really. He just wanted what he wanted when he wanted it. He never waited for *anything*. Not even for her. When he wanted her, he just ... took her.

Sighing, Zora shook her head. It wasn't working. She wasn't going to be able to work up anything resembling anger at him. Because he had never treated her with anything but respect, and care and consideration. If his greatest sin was that he wanted her all the time, and didn't like waiting to have her, then she was in for a hard road to get him and their "fling" out of her system.

"I don't mean to get all in your business or anything," Rashad continued. "But as far as you and him ..."

"Nothing changes," Zora said. "We were just ... kickin' it over Break."

She couldn't even look at him when she said those words, because they felt so blatantly false. But it was basically what she and Deuce had agreed to—the temporary shedding of expectations. And that was all.

"Figured."

"What does that mean?" Zora snapped.

Rashad shrugged, looking away from the road for a moment. "Nothing. I just don't see bruh at a BLM march, do you?"

"It's not like he's oblivious to what's going on out there. He's been stopped before."

Rashad laughed. "*Impressive.* Him, and every other Black man in America. That's hardly the equivalent of street cred."

Zora rolled her eyes. "He's more than you think, Rashad," she murmured. "And besides, that wasn't what it ... what we were about."

"Okay, so tell me," Rashad's voice rose a little, and Zora heard the annoyance, and the jealousy he had concealed before. "What *were* you about?"

"It doesn't matter," she said. "Because ..."

"Did you fuck him?"

"Shad."

"You did, right? Because that's all I can think of that would make someone like that interesting to someone like you. Curiosity about the magic dick that sends all these dumb-ass girls scurrying his way to get used."

Zora's stomach clenched at the phrase, '*sends all the girls scurrying his way.*'

But that was Deuce's rep. And though Rashad hadn't said it, implicit in his comment was some judgment about the type of girls Deuce was notorious for bedding. He generally checked for Latinas and White chicks, and the precious few who weren't, may as well have been since they looked it. His type was so firmly established that even people on campus who had never exchanged three words with him could probably pick his likely sex partners out of a line-up.

Zora knew what it was like to be fetishized. Since puberty there had been guys, some of them White, some of them Black, for whom her darkness, her unmistakable *Blackness*, seemed to be her single most irresistible feature. They stared at her in a manner that was vaguely disturbing, sometimes putting their arm against hers, rhapsodizing about the contrast in their skin tones. Or they played a little too often with her wiry, kinky hair, testing its texture, stretching and releasing it; examining each component of her as though she was a rare museum piece.

Deuce wasn't like that.

He never remarked on their differences, but instead, often told her she was beautiful, or pretty. Even Rashad had never done that—leaned in, though they were in a crowded room, in a Target checkout line, or waiting for movie tickets—and with mouth against her ear, whispered, *you're so beautiful* or *damn, you look amazing today.*

Where'd you learn that? Zora had asked him once. *Where did you learn to make a girl feel so good?*

But that time, she meant something else entirely. Deuce had been at the foot of the bed, between her legs. When he lifted his head, he looked dizzy, and drunk with her. Sliding up along her body, he was rock-hard.

Making you feel good, makes me feel good, he said almost matter-of-factly. *And you don't know, Zee ... you taste better than anything in this world.*

Then he kissed her, long and deep so she could taste herself as well. But Zora still didn't know what he was talking about. To her, what made the kiss good, was just ... him.

"You know what?" Rashad said now. "It don't matter. You fucked him, but it's over. That's the important thing. It's over. And I'm *confident* in my shit ... Fuck that nigga."

Shad almost never used the word 'nigga.' On principle, he avoided it, believing that the argument that Blacks had somehow 'reclaimed' it was nonsense. That was how Zora knew he wasn't even close to being over this news of her and Deuce.

"SO, we're hoping to have L.A. finalized by spring," Zora said. "A huge rally, and refocusing of the movement, so that people know we're still here, and still keeping the pressure on."

"That's Spring Break though," Mia said.

"Yeah, but I've never been to L.A. so I'm cool with it. Can we count you in?"

"Nope. You know I need to go get my tan on."

Zora rolled her eyes. Mia had been her freshman year roommate and they remained close, but she was more an ally of the movement than an active participant. If Zora told her they needed bodies in a room, Mia could be counted upon to mobilize her sorors, but she wasn't exactly a dedicated adherent to BLM.

Right now, Mia was lying on Zora's bed watching her as she folded and put away laundry. They hadn't talked about It, but Zora knew they would. Mia was simply waiting for a decent length of time shooting-the-breeze-about-meaningless-shit to pass before she pounced.

It had been three days since Zora returned to campus with Rashad, but Mia and most everyone else had just gotten there that afternoon when the dorms reopened. It was Saturday, and classes resumed Monday. Most of the morning, and still now,

Zora was on edge. Deuce's calls and texts had only just stopped coming the evening before, and she already missed them though she had been trying to convince herself she should be relieved. She hadn't responded to any of them, but it made her feel strangely reassured each time she saw that he reached out. It made everything that happened between them more real.

She still hadn't figured out what she would do when she inevitably ran into him on campus, but thankfully she had plenty of other things to occupy her. Rashad had been liaising with a few other BLM chapter heads over Break and they agreed that as a general strategy they wanted to spotlight three instances of excessive force in California, giving the East Coast chapters time to regroup after a spate of bad PR and loss of support.

And according to Rashad, what he called "some dumb-ass state legislator" in California had proposed a Blue Lives Matter bill that would make the shooting of a law enforcement officer a hate crime with enhanced sentencing options.

That gives us something concrete to advocate against, he'd said with excitement in his voice. *A real policy to oppose, instead of some nebulous opposition to excessive force.*

So now, they were working with a group of law students at Stanford—where Rashad would hopefully be in the fall—on alternative legislative language. Thinking about bill language had unexpectedly piqued Zora's interest, and now she was wondering whether she should bite the bullet and declare a major already. Her coursework wasn't *exactly* all over the map. She was on track for a sociology major if she wanted to go that route, but had left the door open for other choices as well. She could even be pre-law, like Rashad, but something about walking lockstep with him yet again, choosing as he chose, didn't sit comfortably with her.

"Okay, I can't do this anymore," Mia said suddenly. She

released a long sigh. "I'm *dying*, girl. Tell me about you and Deuce."

Zora laughed. "I knew you didn't give a crap about anything else I was saying. I was just waiting to see how long you could hold out."

But Zora didn't want to talk about Deuce. Not with her closest friend. Not with anyone.

"How was he?" Mia asked slyly, sitting up.

Turning away so her friend wouldn't see the way she smiled and shut her eyes, Zora continued shoving t-shirts into drawers. Finally composing her expression, she glanced over her shoulder.

"He was cool," she said, shrugging.

Mia gave her a look. "You know that's not what I mean. I mean, how *was* he?"

"I don't know if I feel comfortable ..."

"Oh shut up! How many times have we broken niggas down? I want to know, and I think even more than that, I deserve to know."

"Deserve to know?" Zora laughed. "How do you figure that?"

"I was there the first night, remember? If I hadn't forced you to come with me and Sophie over to his table, you never would've even met."

"I don't know whether to thank you. Maybe I should actually be kicking your ass for that," Zora said, shaking her head.

"Was it that bad?" Mia asked softly, grimacing.

Shaking her head, Zora looked at her friend. "No," she said. "It was that good."

Mia's eyes grew saucer-like in size. "Oh shit! Tell me. Tell me *everything*, Zora."

She told her some, but not everything. Some things about

her time with Deuce were much too intimate for public consumption. And others were just too precious.

When she was done, Mia stared at her with something close to sympathy in her eyes. She shook her head and then came over to hug Zora, resting her chin on her shoulder.

"Damn, girl. I knew you shouldn't have messed with him."

Zora pulled back and looked at her incredulously. "Are you serious? You said exactly the opposite, Mia!"

"Since when you listen to me? That was like playing with fire. And now that you're back at school, when you see him with all those girls, your ass is damn sure going to get burned."

"WHAT YOU UP TO RIGHT NOW?"

Zora looked up into Rashad's eyes and offered him a smile and a shrug. They had just delivered the news of their plan to the members, and it had been well-received. Some of them committed to try to make it to L.A. for the rally, and others said they would help spread the word. Rashad was planning to find sponsors to pay for him and Zora as co-chairs, and about five others to make the trip, all expenses included. He was in high spirits because the meeting had gone well, but Zora hadn't been able to muster up any enthusiasm for just about anything lately.

Four days. They had been back in classes for four days, and Deuce's attempts to get in touch had officially come to a halt. She was beginning to feel like an idiot—an idiot for wanting him to try, and an even bigger idiot for planning to ignore him if he did.

"No plans," Zora said, letting Rashad help her gather her laptop and notes, and shove them into her backpack.

"Then come get a burger with me," he said inclining his

head toward the door. And when she hesitated, he smiled. "No strings, no agenda. I promise. Just a burger."

Zora nodded. "Sure."

They went to a pub-style restaurant on the edge of campus, where they were lax about checking ID, so Zora ordered a beer to go with her blue-cheese burger and fries. Rashad didn't drink alcohol, so he asked for a Coke with his food, though Zora could see him forming questions in his mind, and judgments about her wanting to drink.

When they were together, she scarcely did. Because he didn't drink at all, and it wasn't that important to her, she had just naturally abstained when they went out to eat. The fact that she hadn't done so now, she knew, would cause him to draw all kinds of conclusions. The only accurate conclusion would have been that she liked the sharp taste of beer with salty foods like french fries. It was no deeper than that.

"It's weird not seeing you every day," Rashad said when their waitress left them alone again.

"It's weird for me, too," Zora said honestly.

"Weird-good, or weird-bad?"

"Weird weird." She shrugged. Her eyes filled, and her vision became blurred.

Rashad reached across the table and held her hand, leaning in. "Hey. What's the matter? Tell me what's going on."

Zora shook her head and tugged her hand away, blotting the corner of her eyes with her fingertips. "It's just ... I don't know if you know, and I don't know how to tell you that ..." Her throat clogged, so she cleared her throat and started again. "You're one of the most important people in my life, Shad. Like, *ever*."

Rashad's face softened and he grabbed her hand again. "I know that, Zora. I mean, that's what I've been saying. A woman like you. That's like my destiny. So, we should ..."

Zora sat up straight, suddenly clear-headed once again.

"Stop," she said, leaning back in her seat. "Don't say anymore. I don't think you're understanding me."

"What am I not understanding?"

"I'm not ... saying this because I want us to get back together, Shad. I'm saying it because ... because we *won't* get back together. And I just wanted you to know that even so, you've been important to me. You helped me grow and figure out so many things about myself. And for that I can't even begin to ..."

"Don't say it. Don't say, '*I can't begin to thank you*', Zora. Just ... don't. I wasn't your fucking academic *advisor*. I was your man." He looked away from her and shook his head. "I can't believe this shit. Are you getting all weepy because you're over there strung out over some *other* nigga? And feeling guilty about it? Is that wh ..."

"Shad, we're not like a couple anymore. And we hadn't been for a long time. It doesn't have anything to do with anyone else. I mean, are you even in love with me?"

"*Of course I am!* What do you think I was trying to say?" His voice was an angry whisper.

"But you didn't. You didn't say that."

Rashad looked at her, his expression exasperated. "I have said it, Zora. A million times since we got together. And if it makes you happy, I'll say it a million more times."

"It wouldn't make me happy, because it's not true. Just now? Do you know what you said to me? You said that a woman *like me* was your destiny. You didn't say *I* was your destiny. It isn't even about me at all. It's about the image you have in your head of the kind of woman who fits into your picture for your life.

"And I don't blame you for that, because I have a picture too. And you're the one who helped me paint it. That's what I was trying to say. That you helped me picture *my* path. And that's what was so beautiful about us ..."

Rashad's face softened once again. "You helped me, too," he said finally. "We were a good team."

"We *are* a good team," Zora said. "But just not ..."

"Yeah. I know." He leaned back in his seat and looked at her, a sad smile on his face.

"Do you hate me now?" she asked softly.

He shook his head, squeezed her hand. "I could never hate you, Zora."

"And I could never stand it if you did."

Smiling a smile that was just the tiniest bit sad, Rashad leaned in and pulled Zora toward him across the table. And they kissed, a sweet kiss of closure.

Just then, they heard a shout of raucous laughter and turned toward it, breaking apart. A few tables away, Deuce's friend Kaleem sat, sharing a joke with two girls. And as they looked on, Deuce emerged from the back of the pub where the restrooms were, to join them. Reaching into his back pocket to first pull out his wallet, he slid in next to one of the girls, who was busty with strawberry blonde hair and too much lipstick for a weekday.

Seeing him made Zora's heart lurch, and then race. He looked really good, wearing a charcoal grey long-sleeved t-shirt and washed out, slightly baggy jeans. Only seeing him now did she realize just how much she had missed him. And that was saying something, since she already knew she missed him *a lot*. While her eyes were still on him, he reached for his jacket which had been slung over the back of his chair and shrugged it on.

"This town is just too damn small," Rashad muttered. "You want to leave?"

Zora shook her head numbly. "No." She watched as a waitperson brought Deuce and his party the bill. As the server was about to duck away again, Deuce held her wrist and handed her the credit card with the slip. "Looks like they're about to. And anyway ... it's no big deal," she lied.

Zora turned to look at Rashad and he had a wry look on his face. Sipping his water, he leaned back in his seat yet again.

"Human relationships," he said, sounding resigned. "They're complicated."

TEN

"*Damn*, man! Are you *already* lit?"

Deuce opened his door to admit Kaleem and their dates for the evening. Blinking, he grinned at his friend. "Just a little head-start. Good evening, ladies."

He gave a little bow to Tamara and Lisa, two of his and Kaleem's stand-bys—chicks who were always willing and available for some good, old-fashioned no-strings fun. Tamara was his, if one could call her that. Tall and leggy, she looked destined to be on the pages of a men's magazine posing in a beer ad, wearing short-shorts and a much-too-small tank top. She was pretty, but in an obvious, almost pedestrian way that Deuce had lately come to think of as boring.

"I missed you," she said, kissing him on the lips. Her mouth tasted waxy from the lip-stain she was wearing, and Deuce had to force himself not to wipe it off.

"Ready to roll?" he asked, grabbing his keys.

"Roll?" Kal laughed. "Hell nah we ain't drivin' with your drunk ass. We about to hoof it over there. It's not that cold."

"I'm not hoofin' it *anywhere*," Deuce said.

"I haven't been drinking," Lisa said, snatching the keys from between his fingers. "I'll drive tonight."

Kal shrugged, and looked at Deuce for confirmation.

"Yeah. Cool," he said. "Let's go."

The party was the first big one since Winter Break, and he needed it. He'd only been back one week and it had been pretty crappy to begin with, culminating in yesterday's run-in with Zora. Well, it wasn't accurate to call it a run-in since he hadn't been witness to it himself. But Kal had given him a vivid picture to stew on while he was alone in his room at night.

According to Kal, when he was in the men's room at Mulvane's Zora had come in with Rashad Dixon and after what looked like a very animated and emotional conversation, they had kissed. *Kissed.* Just hearing about it, and then thinking about it—over, and over and *over* again—after the fact made Deuce feel like putting his hand through a wall.

He'd been pissed enough to almost call her again. But he'd done that for five days straight after she left Jersey, and to no avail. She didn't want to see him. It was as simple as that. After all the time they spent together, after New Year's Eve ... after everything, she didn't want to see him.

And so he had to leave it at that.

Or at least try to leave it at that. Because that was the deal. Except he couldn't recall anything about her cutting him off. He thought they would at least be ... friends? Hell, even that sounded implausible. So maybe she thought it best for them both to have a clean break. Truth was, he had been flying by the seat of his pants when he suggested they '*shed expectations and enjoy each other.*' He didn't even know what the hell that meant. In the moment, all he wanted, all he had been asking for was for her to leave all their baggage behind and just be.

Part of what made yesterday so messed up was that Kal didn't even know what happened over Break. Deuce hadn't told a single soul. And the only reason Kal mentioned seeing Zora at all was because he was ruminating on how *he* had missed his chance with her. Keeping it all in after that, not telling even his closest friend what was going on, had literally driven Deuce to drink.

Since it was Thursday and he had no classes on Fridays, he started early. And now that it was Saturday, his only plan was to continue drinking, dry out on Sunday for class on Monday and then start the whole routine over again. He figured that after a few weeks of that treatment, he would have detoxed Zora right out of his system.

"You ready to go?" Lisa asked.

Deuce realized he was standing at his door, staring into space, and everyone was looking at him strangely, most especially Lisa. Lisa, a petite blonde who was on the women's track team and met Kal while working out, was actually a cool chick. Sometimes Deuce felt badly for her because he knew she had genuine feelings for Kal, who was only playing around until he found "his queen." If she had a chance, Lisa would probably want to date Kal openly, bring him home to meet the family, make plans for time spent together during school breaks, and the whole nine.

Lately, Deuce had begun to wonder how many 'Lisas' he had discarded in his own social life. He glanced briefly at Tamara, checking her lipstick in the mirrored wall of the elevator as they rode down, and hoped she wasn't actually a 'Lisa.' Damn, he really *was* drunk.

The party was at an off-campus house, where most of the parties for Black students were held. And as usual, he and Kal garnered some nasty looks when they entered with Lisa and Tamara. *Why*, the stares seemed to ask, *would you bother coming to a Black Caucus party if you're just going to turn around and bring a White girl?*

Lisa was White, but Tamara was not. She just *looked* like she was.

Deuce almost laughed. What would happen if he just went up to the deejay, shut off the music and yelled: *She's not White! I swear she's not! She just likes to hang out with White* girls, *and Black* dudes!

"You straight, man?" Kal was looking at him with concern, so Deuce realized he'd done it again—drifted off into space, probably staring with a completely vacant and intoxicated expression on his face.

"Yeah, I'm good," he said. "Lemme just go grab a beer."

Kal put a firm hand on his shoulder. "Nah. Just chill right here a minute."

Deuce decided not to argue, and instead surveyed the room. Penn State's Black population was relatively paltry, so just about every one of the faces was familiar to him, except for some who were probably freshmen. As he scanned, he felt his spirits plummet. He didn't know why he thought this was a good idea. Two minutes in, and the scene was getting old.

Next to him, Lisa and Tamara were swaying to the loud music. He watched Lisa for a while, gamely enduring the dirty looks, bopping a little off-beat. She didn't just like Kal a lot, Deuce decided, she was stone *in love* with the brother. Why else would she put up with being in a place where ninety percent of the women were looking at her with open hostility, and seventy-five percent of the dudes saw her as an object of either prey, or pity?

Damn. Kal was a real asshole. And so, he realized now, was he.

———

"*OH SHIT.* Do you want to go?"

Mia clutched Zora's arm and turned to stand in front of her, as though hoping to block from view what Zora had already seen. Across the room, flanked by two girls—one blonde and tiny; and the other tall and brunette—was Deuce. He was scowling, and not looking like he was particularly enjoying himself, but the girls with him sure were. The brunette danced next to him, occasionally brushing her ass against his leg and lifting her arms in the air, whipping her hair back and forth in a manner that seemed a little desperate and attention-hungry.

Zora should have felt good about the fact that Deuce didn't seem to notice her at all, but she didn't. The girl was *brushing her ass against him*, after all. Something inside her chest turned white-hot.

"No, don't be stupid," she told Mia. "I'm going to have to see him sometime. In fact, I think I should just get it over with and go say 'hello.'"

"Wait. What now? Girl, *no*. You have a look on your face like you're about to cut a bitch."

Zora laughed, bitterly. "I don't do shit like that."

Mia sighed. "And you don't generally use words like 'shit' either, but here you go, *cussing*, so ... Rashad said he was stopping through, right? I say we just get a drink and wait right here. I'm sure he'll be ..."

"I'm going right now," Zora said, ignoring Mia. "I'm just going to go talk to him."

With a few wide and purposeful steps, she crossed the room, skirting around the people in her path, eyes fixed on Deuce. She was only a few feet away when he spotted her.

For a moment, his eyes lit up—as much as they could anyway—but it was clear to Zora, the closer she got, that he was drunk. Not falling-down-and-sloppy drunk, but definitely within three-drink range of that stage.

When she was almost directly in front of him, Zora saw his

throat bob as he swallowed. And then she saw *that look* on his face. The one she had almost forgotten, though it was very recently that she had last seen it. It was the same look he gave her on New Year's Eve when she first came out of the guest room at his father's house, wearing her white dress—a mixture of pride, and raw desire. Seeing that look now, Zora softened toward him for a nanosecond, and almost forgot why she was annoyed until the brunette reminded her, by slinging an arm around Deuce's neck, pulling him down to say something into his ear.

He seemed only dimly aware that the girl was there at all, because his eyes were still fixed on Zora, as hers were on him.

"Hi," she said when they were standing in front of each other, less than a foot apart. Her tone was defiant.

The brunette looked at her and then at Deuce, but stood aside as though realizing that something above her pay-grade was about to happen.

"Hey," he said, in that unexpectedly deep timbre of his.

Even with the music and noise around them, Zora could hear him perfectly, as though only his voice alone could penetrate the chaos and enter her consciousness. Just over her shoulder, she sensed Mia hovering.

"I just thought I'd come over and say 'hello'," she said. "Since I haven't seen you, since ..."

"Yeah," he said, nodding. "New Year's Day. I tried to reach you, but ..."

"It doesn't matter anymore," Zora said, struggling to sound breezy. "Since you're clearly ... back in the saddle." She let her eyes drift briefly toward the brunette.

Deuce's eyes narrowed a little. "I called, and texted. I even went by your house and your brother told me you left. I've been *trying* to reach you ..."

"You tried for barely a week. And now you're here, so ..."

"For barely a ... Zee, you can't be ..."

"Serious? Yeah, I kind of am."

She knew she was being unfair, but her body had been occupied by a little alien, green monster. She wasn't in control of what she said or did any longer.

Now Deuce's eyes weren't narrowed. He opened them wider. "You're *unbelievable*. Y'know that? You know how ..."

"Hey, Zora. Look, Rashad just got here!"

Mia's hand on her arm, firmly, almost painfully diverted her attention from Deuce for a moment and Zora looked at her friend, grateful that she had short-circuited what was sure to be a very messy scene.

"I have to go," she said, giving Deuce one last look. "I just wanted to say hi. Enjoy your night."

Spinning on her heel, she barreled in the general direction of the front door where Mia was leading her. As far as she could tell, Rashad was nowhere in the vicinity, but she was glad to have been saved from herself.

"Jesus, what the hell was *that*?" Mia asked her, when they were standing just outside the front door. "Don't turn into one of those messy-ass chicks, Zora. For real."

It was cold, and people kept brushing by them, entering and exiting the crowded house. Zora rubbed her hands together and shook her head.

"I know. You were right. I shouldn't have even gone over there to talk to him. I don't know what I was ... We should just ... We should go."

"Your coat," Mia said. "My coat. They're still inside."

"I don't want to go back in there. Could you ...?"

"Of course. Wait here, okay? *Don't* move. Just wait."

While Mia went back in, Zora stood on the front porch, stomping her feet and rubbing her hands together. God, that was embarrassing. She *would* have made a scene. If Mia hadn't come to the rescue, maybe she would have for-real cut a bitch.

"How the hell did I let this happen to me?" she asked herself aloud.

"How the hell did you let *what* happen to you?"

Zora spun at the familiar voice and almost threw her arms around Rashad. Safe, sensible, never-made-her-lose-her-mind Rashad. He was just getting there, his hat pulled down over his ears, and the collar of his jacket turned up.

"And why you standin' out here in the cold with no coat?" He looked even more confused, pulling her closer and rubbing his hands up and down her arms.

"It's a long ..."

"Zee!"

"No ..." She took two steps backward and out of Rashad's embrace. "Not now ... Deuce, *no*."

Like her, he was without a coat.

"What d'you mean *no*?" he demanded. "What was that ... inside? What ..."

Rashad stepped between them, blocking Deuce's path to her, putting both his hands up. "She said no, chief."

"*Chief?*" Deuce gave a harsh bark of laughter. "Who the fuck ... man, you better back the hell up."

"No," Rashad said, his voice calm.

He had about an inch in height on Deuce, but Deuce was much more powerfully-built. Zora felt the coiled tension coming in waves off them both.

"Rashad," Zora said to his back, her voice quavering. "It's fine. We were talking inside, and ..."

"You told him no, so you need to stand your ground, and he needs to leave you the hell alone," Rashad said.

"Don't tell her what she *needs* to do." Deuce took a step forward so that now, he and Rashad were squaring off, mere inches apart. "You ain't got nothin' to do with this. This is between me and Zora."

Just then Mia emerged from the house, wearing her coat, and with Zora's draped over her arm. She looked wildly from Rashad to Deuce and then at Zora.

"There is no 'you and Zora.' She's done with you, son," Rashad said, leaning in, his voice scornful. "Your ass was just fun-and-games ... playtime."

"Oh, for real?" Deuce said, almost sweetly. *"How 'bout you and me have some playtime, muthafucka?"*

And in as little time as it took Zora to blink, Deuce made a sudden ducking motion, head-butting Rashad directly in the face. Then Mia was screaming, a group of guys Zora didn't know were saying, *'whoa, whoa,* whoa!' charging toward the action, and shoving her out of the way. Behind the phalanx of broad-shouldered guys, Zora saw nothing, but heard grunts and the sounds of a scuffle. By the time the mass of bodies in front of her parted enough for her to get a view of what was going on, there was blood everywhere.

Rashad and Deuce were held apart by two other guys, while they yelled at each other, kicking and struggling to be set free. Deuce looked relatively no-worse-for-the-wear except for the expression of almost rabid rage on his face. But Rashad wasn't as lucky. His nose and mouth were a mass of dark crimson, blood streaming from his nose, frothing from his mouth, and spraying onto the front of his coat while he screamed expletives. Deuce's face looked fine, but the blood spatter had made its way down the front of his shirt as well.

While Zora looked on in stunned horror, Mia dragged her by the arm away from the house and down the front path into the street.

"OH MY GOD, Shad, you look ... awful."

Zora was sitting next to the examining table in Health Services, a hand on Rashad's thigh. His nose had swollen to twice its size, both his eyes were ringed in purple, and his upper lip had been split along the middle. The consensus from the sleepy nurse practitioner and LPN who had initially attended to him was that he would need two small stitches just inside his upper lip, but everything else would be fine with a few extra-strength Tylenol, a bag of ice and the passage of time.

After Mia dragged her away from the mêlée, and back to her room where Zora paced a hole in the rug, she waited about a half hour before calling Rashad's cellphone. He picked up eventually, and explained that the brawl had broken up fairly quickly after Deuce's friend Kaleem arrived on the scene to calm him down. And he had gotten a ride over to University Health Services to take care of his injuries.

"I've been in scraps a lot worse than this," Rashad said. He sounded like he was talking around his lips rather than between them. "I'll be fine."

Zora grimaced and touched his thigh. "I am *so* sorry. I shouldn't have ..."

"Not your fault," Rashad said. But he was saying the words by rote, and not with any real sincerity, which Zora could not say she blamed him for.

"It *is* my fault. I saw him inside, and I shouldn't have ... engaged with him. I just ..."

"But you are," Rashad said. "*Engaged* with him."

"Just ... stop talking. It hurts me to see you do it," Zora said squeezing his leg.

"I will. But lemme just say this one thing ..."

Zora held her breath.

"He's not for you, Zora." Rashad shook his head. "And this ain't even about me and you. He's going to get you off-track ..."

"It's not ..."

"Don't say it's not that deep," Rashad said, raising his voice to speak over her. Then he put a hand to his mouth as though in pain. "I don't think even *you* believe that."

Zora looked away. "We only spent a little over a week together."

"Yeah. And look where 'a little over a week' got you. Already." Rashad shook his head and then looked up at the ceiling.

Before Zora could respond, the LPN returned to the room, and slid a metal instrument tray closer to the examining table. Smiling grimly, she looked at Rashad.

"I won't lie to you, young man," she said. "This isn't going to be pleasant. Not one bit."

———

WHEN ZORA MADE it back to her dorm, it was well past two a.m. but she felt like she'd been up for three days. Apart from a few couples sitting around in the common room, hovering over but barely touching each other, as if deciding whether and where to continue the mating dance, things were quiet. Her legs were heavy, and walking down the hallway toward her room seemed like more than she could handle. She wondered whether Mia was awake. She didn't feel like being alone with her thoughts, and despite being tired, wasn't sure she would be able to sleep.

After his stitches were done, she'd gone with Rashad back to his apartment where he insisted he didn't need her to stick around. Zora could see in his eyes that he was angry with her, and with himself as well, probably. This was not the kind of drama he got involved in. Not Rashad Dixon. And given how small their little community was, there was every likelihood people were already spreading the news about how Rashad Dixon had thrown down with Deuce Scaife at the first party of the semester.

He's not for you, Zora.

Rashad's words were still ringing in her ears. They shouldn't have shaken her the way they did, because it was what she had been telling herself all this time. It was what made it possible for her to leave his father's house and ignore his calls and text messages afterwards. But as the days went by, and the silence between them lengthened, her resolve was shaken.

The idea that they were so different was beginning to seem like someone else's idea.

Maybe Rashad's voice was the one in her head that had been telling her that all along; his and that of their community of activists whose standards for themselves and the world at large sometimes seemed impossible to meet. The reasons for Zora's avoidance of almost all Rashad's calls over the holidays hadn't only been about their breakup. It had also been about that first call, the one that came when she and Deuce were sitting in The Cheesecake Factory.

Their food had only just arrived and Zora looked down at her way-too-large portion of fries with satisfaction, then up at Deuce who was smiling at her. She thought he looked a little nervous, like it was a first date, and she was thinking that it wouldn't be so bad if it were, because not only was he handsome, but he had been so solicitous with her, and so respectful. Everything she had heard about him was at odds with how he treated her. She thought about the little twist of excitement in her stomach when she first heard from him that morning, and how that twist became almost a lurch once she saw him.

And she puzzled over it, because she and Deuce Scaife had had a *one-night stand* and that was *all* it was supposed to be.

And she puzzled over the fact that she hadn't felt that kind of excitement in a long time about anyone; not just sexual excitement, though there was that. But excitement at getting to know him. The last person she'd felt that for was Rashad himself.

And yet once the phone rang, and she saw that it actually *was* Rashad, she was almost angry at him for the intrusion into a moment that she wanted to be all her own. Since she met him, there had been very little that was all her own, and here he was again, when she was with someone she liked and was very much attracted to, crowding into her thoughts, and making her second-guess them. For the first time ever, in that moment, Rashad felt like someone who was taking something from her, rather than giving.

Zora had barely been at the university for a month before she met him. He was the booming presence at the front of the room during her first Black Caucus meeting. Zora still remembered his admonition that they not allow their lesser numbers (*"I refuse to use the phrase minority!"*) relegate them to second-class citizenship. And that they make up for what they lacked in numbers on campus by amplifying their voice, delivering a powerful message, and always speaking truth to power.

He reminded Zora of a fiery preacher standing up there, and she could tell that much of what he said he had probably planned, or even rehearsed. But that didn't lessen the appeal. In fact, it increased it, because it meant that he was earnest in his desire to motivate and mobilize the new freshman class; that he cared enough to think about and then deliver heartfelt, prepared remarks.

After the meeting was over, Rashad was mobbed by people who wanted to meet him one-on-one, mostly girls who smiled shyly and rocked back and forth on their feet. Zora watched from the sidelines, waiting until the crowd thinned before making her own approach. There was only one other person with him when she finally plucked up the courage. Her voice croaked when she said hello, and Rashad smiled at her, his eyes kind.

It was only a month after that when they became a couple, and about five weeks later they slept together for the first time. Rashad waited before initiating anything because—he told her later—he wanted her to "feel safe."

And she had, with him. He was such a larger-than-life sheltering presence. Just being with him had helped define her. No one had to ask what Rashad Dixon's girl was about. Except now that she was no longer Rashad Dixon's girl, did it mean she needed to revisit the question? *What* was *she about?*

ELEVEN

"Yo! You *smashed*? You and *Zora*?"

Kaleem was pacing Deuce's room, both hands resting on the dome of his head, eyes wide.

"Shut up, man. It wasn't even about that."

"Tell me then. What was it? Because I'm about to fight you my-damn-self. That's foul as hell, man. You knew I was tryna push up ..."

"I told you, it wasn't about that!"

Kal stopped pacing and stared at him. "What was it about then?" Deuce said nothing and Kal nodded. "Thought so. And I *know* that shit was good. Had to be, the way you just kirked on ol' boy. And with Tamara there too? Watching you fight over some *other* chick? That shit was just ... cold."

"Kaleem, shut the fuck up."

"What happened? She boyfriend-bombed you? Man, I *been* told you her and Rashad ..."

"I need to talk to her." Deuce pushed himself up from his bed. But the floor felt rubbery and less than solid. The next thing he knew, Kal was at his side, holding him up.

"Whoa, man. Chill. I think whatever the fuck you drank is finally kickin' in."

"I gotta talk to her tonight, Kal ..."

"No, man. Listen to me. She will not want to see your ass. Although, no lie ... I heard that shit was impressive. Just *head-butted* that nigga ..."

Kal was right. Zora wouldn't want to see him.

But he had to go anyway. Because if she slept on it, she would only wake up angrier. That was how stuff like this worked. Time only amplified it, and the rumors would only make it worse. By the time the story made the rounds a few times, it would have him standing over Rashad Dixon with a pickax about to bury it in his head.

"I need to get over there. But ..."

Kal looked at him blankly. "But ... what?" Then he was shaking his head. "*Hell* nah. You want me to go with you? And do what? Hold your tissue while you cry and beg at her door?"

"You're a real ..."

"Hey." Kal held his hands up. "I *did* my part. You got lucky tonight with your drunk ass. If I hadn'ta stepped in when I did, you would've been laid the fuck out. *He* was sober."

Deuce blinked and shook his head. "So you really gon' let me walk out in the cold, and find my way ..."

"You're not that drunk, and it ain't that far," Kal said. "Just try to walk in a straight line. When this shit you about to do blows up in your face, I ain't tryna be there to catch no shrapnel."

"Y'know what, Kal? Fuck you."

Kaleem laughed. "You're welcome."

Shrugging on his coat, Deuce made his way slowly toward the door, getting his bearings as he went. Once outside his room, he stood at the top of the stairs to the main level and considered; then thinking better of it, he went for the elevators instead. In the mirrored wall, he saw his reflection and groaned.

He looked like crap. His eyes were bloodshot, and one of them looked a little swollen. Reaching up, he tentatively felt to see whether he had been hit. He didn't recall Rashad getting any shots in, but then Deuce had been operating on pure adrenaline and wasn't sure he would remember if he had.

He remembered a fleeting glance at Zora though, and the shock on her face. He remembered her girl, Mia, pulling her away and then Kal showing up to help break things up. And he remembered Tamara, crying, her makeup streaking down her face, and the look in her eyes of hurt and humiliation.

He never wanted to be that guy again. The one who would make a girl look like that.

Outside, the cold woke him up a little bit. There was no snow on the ground, but a little ice, from freezing rain they'd had earlier in the day. It crunched under his feet as he walked. Deuce navigated the patches of visible ice slowly and carefully, and thought his luck had to have changed when he made it to Zora's dorm without winding up on his ass. But the door was locked, and so he had to stand outside in the cold for almost a half-hour before someone showed up and let him in behind them, giving him a semi-suspicious once-over but saying nothing.

"I go here," he said. His speech sounded garbled.

Maybe Kal was right, and he should have waited. Zora would be horrified when she saw him like this. That is, if she even opened the door long enough to see him at all.

Finally upstairs, he stood there for a few seconds then raised a fist and knocked. Inside, there was no sound. She was probably sleeping. If she was there at all. Maybe she was with Rashad, nursing his wounds, apologizing ... consoling him. Deuce closed his eyes at the thought, just as the door opened.

Zora was standing there, barefoot, in shorts and a tank. Her hair was secured with a scarf, all of it concealed beneath the colorful fabric. For a few beats she just looked at him, taking him in from head to toe, saying nothing. Her lips trembled and her eyes filled, and then with both hands she shoved him hard in the center of his chest.

Deuce staggered backwards into the hall, feeling his own eyes fill.

"Why the hell did you *do that?*" she demanded. "What is *wrong* with you?"

Taking two steps toward her, he shook his head, saying nothing.

"He had to get stitches!" she screamed at him. "Do you know that? He ..." She raised her hands to push him again, but Deuce grabbed her wrists and walked toward her until they were both in her room. Then, reaching blindly behind him with one hand, the other still holding one of her wrists, he shoved the door shut.

Looking around, he confirmed that she was alone.

"No, he's not here!" Zora yelled at him, prying loose. "He had to go to Health Services. Because of *you*. Because of what *you* did!"

"I'm sorry," he croaked.

"No, you're not!"

Deuce looked at the floor, thinking for a moment, then looking up at her again. "I'm sorry I upset you," he amended.

Zora's shoulders sagged. "And you say *I'm* unbelievable?" She turned away from him, putting both her hands over her face.

Deuce moved closer, walking into her, so his chest was against her back. He lowered his head, burying his face into the top of her scarf-covered head, inhaling the scent of coconut and almonds, feeling Zora's head fall back. He lifted a hand, touching her at first hesitantly, waiting to see if she objected, resting it on her stomach and pulling her back, tighter against him.

"Missed you," he breathed. Bowing his head further, he buried his face in the crook between her neck and shoulder and was grateful when he felt her slight tremble.

This. They always had at least this—the involuntary responses of their bodies to each other. Zora made a sound of frustration and tried to pull away but Deuce tightened his hold around her waist, keeping her in place against him.

"Tell me you missed me," he said. But it sounded like a plea. Kal was right. He was begging.

Zora twisted again, trying to get away, but this time half-heartedly, and finally weakening.

"I'm *sorry*, Zee," he said. "*I'm sorry.*"

"Deuce, you can't ... you can't *do* stuff like that." But she wasn't screaming anymore, and no longer sounded angry.

Finally, Zora turned to look at him. And for the first time that night, he saw the softness in her eyes that he had so quickly come to yearn for. She lifted a hand to his left eye, where he was now fairly certain he had taken a blow.

"You look ..." She didn't finish the sentence, but instead let her head fall forward and rest on his chest, just beneath his chin. "I missed you, too," she said instead.

Deuce exhaled and pulled her tighter against him, feeling her finally relax into his embrace.

———

THEY SLEPT WRAPPED around each other, but it was a fitful restive sleep. Deuce opened his eyes whenever Zora moved, and when he did, saw that her eyes were open too. It seemed only minutes passed though it had to be hours.

Morning light broke. Zora got up and Deuce sat up as well. But she was only going to close the blinds and then joined him once again on the small bed.

When he tried to pull her against him spoon-fashion, Zora instead faced him, and offered a small, wan smile. She draped an arm across his middle, and he did the same to her, both of them simply wanting to know that even if they slept, the other would still be there. A hundred things remained unspoken, that they would no doubt talk about later. But for now, exhaustion won out and their weary eyes finally shut, and stayed that way.

A TIGHTNESS, and solid mass of discomfort around his left eye was the most significant sensation Deuce felt when he woke up. That, and a vague but persistent pounding on the side of his head. His right side was numb, and when he tried to move, he realized it was because Zora was asleep on his arm. Stretching and flexing his right hand, he tried to get the circulation going without having to move her, but the motion caused her to awaken. She looked dazed, and still exhausted. He was too. But he was glad to be exactly where he was.

Taking a deep breath, Zora tried to sit up but Deuce clamped a hand on her hip.

"Morning," he said. His voice was gravelly with sleep.

"Morning," she returned. "This ... I hope you know this doesn't mean I'm not mad as hell at you."

"I know."

She rubbed her eyes, and yawned. Her breath was slightly stale, but strangely, that didn't lessen her appeal. Not even a little bit.

"I'm hungry," she said.

"You're always hungry."

"Don't ... don't be cute right now," she warned. "Nothing about last night was cute. So don't go trying to be cute now."

"Maybe we can make it to breakfast," he offered.

"Lunch."

"Lunch?" Deuce glanced over his shoulder and back at her desk where her digital clock sat. It was past one in the afternoon.

"Let's shower, and then we can go eat."

They showered together. An infraction that could have gotten Zora kicked out of the dorm. Standing together in the stall, they washed each other, soapy hands roaming each other's bodies in a way that was both very sexual, and not sexual at all. Deuce was erect, just seeing her like that, slick and dark, the sheen of her body wash making her glisten.

When she washed him, her hands were tender, lightly skimming the injured parts of his face. Then they stood under the stream and washed the previous evening—or most of it —away.

In the Hub, once they got there, several pairs of eyes followed them as they got their food; there were whispers behind hands, and a few wide-eyed stares. Deuce had gotten a much better look at himself, and it wasn't pretty. His left eye was swollen, though not quite swollen shut, and the whites were white no more, but instead a frightening reddish purple. His vision on that side was blurred, something he would probably have to get checked out to make sure there was no permanent damage.

He and Zora ate in silence at first, but Deuce could feel that the tension between them had lessened. By the time Zora shoved her tray away and sat back, he felt more confident that maybe there was a way forward for them.

"What am I supposed to say to people?" she asked.

Deuce swallowed the mouthful he had been chewing. "What people?"

"Rashad for one. What am I supposed to tell him? After what you did, if we were to ... do this, what would I even say?"

Deuce tried not to show his relief, taking another bite of his burger to mask it.

"*Well?*" Zora demanded. "I mean, you acted like ..."

"You cut me off," he said, finally allowing himself to express his frustration, his anger. "You left Jersey and didn't even tell me. And then when I get here, I see you at some party, and you walk up to me to say 'hi' like nothing even happened?"

"You were with two girls, Deuce, and ..."

"And you were in town making out with Rashad Dixon!"

Zora froze and for a moment looked confused, shaking her head. "No, I wasn ..." And then her eyes lit up with new clarity. "You saw that?"

"No. But I heard about it after. In graphic detail."

She rolled her eyes. "It sounds like the description you got was a little bit faulty, for real. That was nothing. It was ..."

"Okay." He leaned back and folded his arms. "And the girl I was with? That was nothing as well. So, we're even."

"Was it?" Zora asked, looking him in the eye.

"Was it what?"

"Nothing. Was it *nothing?* You and that girl?"

Deuce shrugged. "Yeah. At least last night it was."

Zora bit hard into her lower lip and her nostrils flared.

She was jealous. Just knowing that made him want to cheese. *Hard.* But he contained it and leaned in again.

"Look. I don't need any more action like last night. And I *know* you don't need the drama. So I'ma just lay it out there. I only want you. A'ight? *Just you.* That's what's up."

Zora's eyes softened.

"And if you want, I'll apologize to whatshisname. I won't mean it, but I'll do it if it's what you want."

Zora exhaled an exasperated sigh. "Why wouldn't you mean it? He's never done anything to ..."

"He tried to come between me and you. *That's* what his ass did. So yeah, I'm sorry I made you cry. I'm sorry I embarrassed you. But I'm not sorry I hit him."

Zora rolled her eyes. "I have to work with him ..."

Deuce gritted his teeth.

"... and he's my friend. He's always going to be my friend ..."

He gritted harder.

"So yeah, it would be great if you could ... try to ... manufacture some remorse, and find a way to communicate that to him."

He shrugged. "Okay."

"And then I'm going to need a minute. To ..."

"To what? Figure out how to spin it? So that no one thinks less of you for dumping Rashad Dixon for the likes of me?"

Shaking her head, Zora pursed her lips clearly holding herself back. When finally she spoke, her voice was trembling with anger. "You don't get to talk to me like that. And you don't get to order me up like something on a menu. You might be Christopher Scaife, Jr. but that doesn't mean you get to have whatever you want, whenever you want it. *Especially* after what you did last night."

So, this was to be his punishment. Exile.

"How long?" he asked. "How much time d'you need?"

Zora shook her head. "I don't know."

Deuce tried not to roll his eyes.

So, this was it. This was where he would meet Relationship-Zora. Already, she was shaping up to be much more difficult than Winter-Break-Fling-Zora. But it didn't matter. However he got her, whichever Zora she was, he wanted her.

Sliding his hand across the table, he touched the tips of her fingers with the tips of his.

"Okay." he said. "I'll wait."

TWELVE

"Your movement's seen a steady erosion of support over the last year. Some might even say that it's dead. How would you respond to that?"

The reporter was an earnest-looking young man with bluish-gray eyes and an impressive head of sandy-blonde hair which he had styled into a pompadour. He wore silver rings on three fingers of each hand, and had a piercing in his nose. Just from looking at him, Zora could tell that he was probably the only person at the conservative local paper who even wanted to interview a couple of rabblerousing college kids who rallied around a subject as uncomfortable as police use of excessive force against the Black community.

Rashad looked at Zora before answering, asking with his eyes whether she wanted to field the question. He always did that—made sure that when they were speaking together, he didn't automatically take the lead. Particularly since people were likely to assume he was the leader anyway. Rashad was scrupulously attentive to all the *"isms"*– racism, sexism, ageism ... No one could accuse him of a single one.

Zora shrugged, to indicate that he should take the question if he wanted it.

"First of all, this isn't *my* movement," he began, stroking his goatee thoughtfully. "It isn't even just a Black movement. It's a *human rights* movement that every American should support, no matter your race. Because Black Lives Matter may focus on a very specific strain of the disease, but it's one that we should all want to see eradicated."

That answer caused the reporter to lean in, listening with even more interest now, though the interview was drawing to a close.

"BLM is about the abuse of the power of the state to deprive citizens of their due process—and in some cases, their very lives," Rashad continued. "And when the state takes your life, and says it's justified, there is no redress that's adequate. For anyone.

"White people think this isn't their problem. *Until it is.* But by then, as a society we will have accepted a gradual erosion of standards about what is or isn't appropriate, lawful, or justifi- able for the men and women in law enforcement to do. You see, Rich ..."

That was one of Rashad's tricks. He used people's names a lot, often shortening them to create a false sense of kinship. The reporter, who had introduced himself as Richard Stanley hadn't invited them to call him "Rich" but Rashad did it anyway, because he knew the man would walk away thinking how personable, how approachable, how ... charismatic that BLM activist was. And all that good feeling would somehow make its way into the words and tone "Rich" chose when he filed his story.

Zora tuned out the rest of Rashad's response, taking the opening to glance down at her phone. They had gotten their pictures taken for the paper about an hour earlier, and now the

Q&A was dragging on. She'd conceded the last few questions to Rashad because she had no confidence in her ability to give a coherent response. Something had occurred to her just that morning in the middle of her English seminar, and she was eager to get back to her room to have it either confirmed, or denied.

Fidgeting, Zora wondered whether she should text Mia and have her come over. But Mia ... she was her girl, but there was no way she was going to be able to keep her fat trap shut about something as juicy as this. And honestly, there was only one person she wanted around while she figured this out.

Opening the messaging app, Zora typed out a quick line and, before she had a chance to change her mind, hit 'send'.

"So, Zora." Their interviewer drew her attention back to him. "Your co-chair thinks that the movement has a long future ahead of it. What do you think?"

"Oh, I agree," she said keeping her voice light. "Absolutely. What you're seeing right now with BLM is evolution, not death. We started by mobilizing people in a very visible and vocal way, but now it's time to go into some closed rooms, strategize and build. But yeah, we're not going anywhere."

Shad looked at her and nodded, smiling his agreement. Zora smiled back. Rich noticed the exchange and nodded and smiled himself, a good sign that Rashad had worked his magic very effectively.

"One last thing," he said. "Word on the street is that you two are partners in other ways as well. How about a future there?"

Shad grinned his most charming grin. "Hey. This woman is always gon' be in my life. So yeah, I guess there's a future there, too."

"Coolness." Rich scribbled in his notepad while Zora

glared at Rashad. "Thank you both for all your time today," he said when he looked up again.

After shaking hands, and exchanging a few more pleasantries, Zora and Rashad watched Rich walk away. When he was safely out of earshot, Zora turned, and with folded arms looked up at her ex-boyfriend.

"Why would you say ...?"

Shad laughed. "C'mon Zora. You really want him all in our business? What was I supposed to say? *'Nah man, she dropped my ass for some other dude.'*?"

"No one dropped anyone for 'some other dude.' And I hope that's not the story you're going around co-signing when people ..."

"I don't put my business out there like that. So chill. Besides, what I said was ambiguous. I just wasn't about to get into all that with him."

Sighing, Zora nodded. "Okay, but don't ... feed into that mess."

Shad shrugged. "What mess? I know as much as anyone else. That you're supposedly with some joker but no one actually *sees* you with the joker. All I know is, I hope he don' got you on some DL bullshit, Zora. Because you know all that is ..."

"We're not talking about him," Zora said, shaking her head. "Just know that I got this. Okay?"

It had been three weeks since the fight, and a little less than that since Deuce had been able to make himself seek Rashad out and offer what Shad called "the most half-assed apology" he ever heard for head-butting him and almost breaking his nose. But Rashad, given who he was, wasn't one to involve "the authorities" in things, whether those authorities were the university administration, or the police. So, he had grudgingly accepted the *mea culpa* and agreed to try to move on.

And as for Deuce and Zora; they were talking every day

now, a few times a day; and she sometimes let him come by so they could study together, but there was no more than that. There was only that much because after just three days of silence when she told him she needed time, it was she who was jones'ing for him.

So Deuce came over twice or so a week and lay across her bed to read for his classes while she worked nearby on her papers, or BLM business. Or they sat on opposite ends of her small loveseat, her feet in his lap, while he played with her toes and they watched TV on her small set that otherwise rarely got used. They both did an admirable job of keeping their hands off each other even though Zora could see the strain and frustration on Deuce's face every single time she showed him the door and told him she had to go to bed, and that she planned to do that alone.

"Anyway, you need a ride back to your dorm?"

"Yes. Please. As long as it's without all the commentary."

"Commentary-free," Rashad said, holding his hands up.

A week earlier, there had been almost a foot of snow, as February reasserted herself, reminding them that January wasn't *real* winter. Navigating one's way around campus was an obstacle course of frozen pathways as the snow melted under the late afternoon sun, and re-froze again by seven p.m.

Zora was glad for the ride once Rashad got his car warmed up, and if she admitted it to herself, glad for his company as well. He hadn't changed in his manner towards her at all, considering everything that had gone on, but there were fewer occasions for them to have those epic-ass conversations, and she missed them. He had accepted their breakup now. Zora believed, though he would never say it, that he had even come to realize that she was right, and that he didn't love her the way he used to, and should. They were better off as friends. But managing the terms of their friendship was something they still hadn't figured out just yet.

It would be a while before she lost the impulse to call him every time she read something she knew he might find interesting, or when she saw a program on TV she knew he would want to watch. Zora was attentive to Deuce now, even when she wasn't with him. She navigated their new status much as she did those patches of ice around campus—cautiously, and alert to possible danger. She knew Deuce wanted her—it was the single most significant source of confidence she had in their relationship.

His wanting her had been the centerpiece of their time together over Winter Break. But the only real test of whether or not there was more was to not let him have her in that way. At least not for now. He thought the enforced abstinence was because of the fight, and even joked about it, occasionally trying to tease longer, deeper kisses out of her, or asking whether he was still "on punishment" when she stopped his hand from sliding down from her waist toward her ass.

And maybe it had been his "punishment", at first.

But now, part of Zora wanted to see how long he would hold out, how interested he could remain in a girl who wasn't giving it up. So far, the answer was 'very interested.' He was the one who had established the rhythm for their contact each day, by calling or texting every morning, and then again later in the day, asking whether he could see her, and accepting her response, even when it wasn't what he wanted to hear.

Occasionally, Zora checked up on him, guiltily, furtively, asking casual questions of Mia and Sophie about whether they had seen him on campus, and who with. Mia was happy to play the spy, but Sophie not so much. She was unhappy Deuce had been taken off the market, and unhappier yet because it was Zora who had accomplished it. And it did appear that the word had gotten around, that Deuce Scaife was no longer a single man, and that it was Zora Diallo who had scored the prize. She noticed strange girls' eyes following her with bitter stares at the oddest times and places; girls she didn't know, and whose past liaisons with Deuce she could only guess at, and hoped never to have confirmed.

"Well, look here ... speak of the Devil," Rashad said as he pulled up to the front of Zora's dorm.

None other than Deuce was walking up the path toward the front door, with his hands stuffed into his jeans. He looked back at the car when it pulled up and did a double-take when he saw who was driving, and who the passenger was. And then he waited.

"That who you were texting in the middle of the interview?" Rashad asked.

"It was hardly the middle, Shad. It dragged out for*ever*."

Shaking his head, Shad made a slight scoffing noise. "You did a good job anyway. Especially with that last question. You hit exactly the right note. I think he was fishing to see whether we were nervous about the bad publicity. So ... good job with that."

"Thanks," Zora said, gathering up her bag and pulling her coat closer around her. Now that Deuce had seen her in Rashad's car, she didn't exactly want him to think she was in no hurry to get out of it. "And thanks for the ride."

"Can I kiss you goodbye?" Rashad asked.

Zora glared at him and he laughed.

"Sorry," he said. "I'm messin' wit' you. I just *wish* I could get one last shot at his ass. That's all. And since I can't fight him ..."

"*Thank you*, Rashad," Zora said pointedly as she shoved open the door. "We'll talk later."

She met Deuce halfway up the path and as she looked up

to greet him, he leaned in and kissed her, square on the lips, briefly sliding her the tip of his tongue. Then he pulled away— far too soon, and far too late, because now Zora felt a tiny ignition inside her, like someone had flipped a switch.

"Hey," she said. Her voice trembled a little.

Deuce's tongue snaked over his lower lip. "Hey," he returned. But despite the kiss he didn't look particularly pleased.

It was only then—dummy that she was—that Zora realized that the show was all for Rashad's benefit. She tried not to roll her eyes.

"So, what's up?" Deuce asked as they headed inside. "You said it was urgent."

"Yeah," she said. "Let's go in first."

ONCE IN HER ROOM, Zora was distracted as Deuce shed his coat. Underneath, all he wore was a plain blue Henley. He hardly ever wore anything else besides Henleys, jeans and a rotation of boots. Nothing fancy or flashy, except for shirts like this that hugged his chest, well-defined arms and narrow waist. He was the kind of guy who should never wear a shirt unless he had to because it was fifteen degrees outside.

Shaking her head, Zora refocused. How could she even be thinking stuff like that? Especially considering why she'd called him over. Reaching into her backpack she pulled out a paper bag and tossed it on the bed.

Deuce looked at it, his eyes narrowed.

"Look inside," she prompted. "It's the only way I know how to tell you."

Reaching for the bag, his eyes still on her, Deuce opened it slowly. And when he saw its contents, he let his chin drop to his chest.

"You're kidding me, right?"

Zora shook her head slowly. "No. But I don't know for sure. I'm almost two weeks late. It could just be stress, but I don't know for sure. That's why I got it."

"But ... *when?*" He looked up at her again, his eyes wide.

"Deuce."

"*Fuck*," he said. "New Year's Eve."

"Yeah."

He took a deep breath and looked at the box, then tore it open to read the instructions. "So let's just do this then."

Zora studied his posture, tried to read his face for traces of anger. She knew she wasn't the only one to blame for their carelessness, but she wouldn't have faulted him for being at least ... suspicious. He was Chris Scaife's son. He was *Chris Scaife, Jr.* Unexpected and unplanned pregnancies were probably among the top three calamities his father told him to guard against. That, and scheming young women.

But there was no anger, not even *apprehension* in his features.

"Hey," he said, clearly eager to move things along. "Let's go."

"Like ... like *now?*" Zora asked, still reeling from his lack of an appropriate response.

"Yeah now. Why? You want to wait until you're even more pregnant?"

She shut her eyes. "Don't say that. Don't even joke like that, Deuce!"

"Sorry." He shrugged. "I thought a little humor ..."

"No, no humor. Okay, let's just ... go."

In the communal bathroom, Deuce checked to make sure the coast was clear before dragging Zora into a stall with him. It was crowded with them both in there, and he was looming over her, not even a foot away.

"I'm not doing this with you staring down at me!" she said. "Are you crazy?"

"I thought you might want the ... moral support," he said.

"Morally support me from the other side of the door. Please."

Deuce obliged and reopened the door, stepping outside.

Zora unzipped her jeans and opened the cellophane packet, removing the test. She squatted with it in position and willed herself to pee. Nothing came. Squeezing her eyes shut, she imagined a waterfall, rain ... every version of running water she could conjure up, but nothing helped.

"What's going on in there?" Deuce asked after a few minutes of silence.

"Nothing. That's the problem. Nothing's going on in here," she said, frustrated. "Could you turn on one of the faucets?"

After a moment, Zora heard that he had. Except it was going too fast.

"Turn it down a little. So it sounds more like ...."

And at that moment someone else entered the bathroom and they had to wait while they did their business and left. Deuce turned the faucet down a little so it sounded more like a trickle.

"It's not working!" Zora said.

"Zee. Calm down. Just gimme a sec."

She heard the bathroom door open and then shut, and realized she was alone.

"Deuce? Crap," she muttered. *Where the hell had he gone?*

Then she heard the bathroom door re-open and the sound of running water once again. Zora remained silent and still, not knowing for sure who was out there.

"Okay ... I got something. Open the door."

"Where'd you go?" she asked irritably.

"Open the door. This'll work."

She opened the door a crack, and just long enough for Deuce to hand her a paper cup. It was warm, and filled with water.

"What am I supposed to do with this?" she asked. "Drink it?"

"Put your three middle fingers in it and try to pee again."

"*Ohhhh*. Okay ... but wait. I can't do that and hold the wand at the same time."

"The *what*?"

"The *pee-stick*. I have no place to put the cup of water and hold the stick, and pee at the same time."

"Zee, open the damn door."

She opened it and Deuce crowded in once again, looking impatient with her now.

"Which do you want me to hold?"

She let her head fall to one side. "Which do *you* want to hold?" she asked.

"Gimme the cup," he said.

He held it while Zora squatted, the stick in position between her legs and her other hand in the cup of warm water.

"Good thing you have the muscle strength in your thighs to do that without sitting on that nasty-ass seat, and without holding on," Deuce said, almost to himself.

"Will you be quiet?" Zora hissed. "And don't look at me, or I can't ..."

Deuce looked up at the ceiling and she closed her eyes, taking a deep breath. After a moment, she felt a desultory trickle as she peed on the stick.

Sighing, she let it drip for a few moments then held it, at a loss for what to do with it.

"Give it to me," Deuce said, wearily.

Zora looked at him, hesitating. "Are you ...?"

"Zee, gimme the stick before you have pee running down your leg."

Reluctantly, Zora handed it over and wiped herself clean, dropping the toilet paper and taking the paper cup from Deuce to empty that into the bowl as well. When she looked up, he was still holding the stick like it was the most normal thing in the world.

"How long?" he asked, leaning against the door.

"Three minutes or less." She pulled up her underwear and jeans and leaned against the side of the stall, opposite Deuce.

"What am I looking for?"

"It'll say 'yes' with a plus or 'no' with a minus sign," Zora choked out.

The comedy of errors now over, the gravity of their situation was beginning to set in. She could feel the onset of a tension headache and her throat felt like it was swollen shut with terror. Deuce said nothing, just leaned against the wall, the plastic wand between his thumb and forefinger.

She could not be pregnant. *She could not.* She could not.

She had her entire life ahead of her, and she couldn't derail it for a kid. And she would never have an abortion, and everyone would say she was a gold-digger, and Rashad would look at her like she had three heads and dismiss her as a fool. And ... her parents, God her father most especially. They probably thought she was a virgin, and was waiting for a nice, Muslim boy. And what about her major? She hadn't even declared one yet! If she had a baby, would she even finish her degree?

"Damn. That was quick."

Deuce turned the test toward her.

No. And a minus sign.

Zora felt her shoulders sag in sweet relief, and Deuce was grinning from ear to ear.

"So, what do we do with this?" he asked, holding up the wand.

"Keep it as a souvenir, maybe. A reminder of our supreme stupidity. Our utter, mindless ..."

"Horniness?"

"Carelessness." Zora said snatching the test from him and dropping it in the container meant for feminine hygiene waste.

Once it was deposited, she took another deep breath.

"Oh my God, I feel like ... ugh. *Thank God!*"

She looked up and Deuce was smiling at her.

"What's the matter? Are you going to let us out of here, or were you thinking you might like to hang out in the bathroom a little longer?"

He shook his head, still grinning. "Nah," he said. "It's just that ..."

Zora opened her eyes wide, prompting him to continue.

"... you're just *so freakin' cute.*"

He leaned in and kissed her, long and hard, hands braced against the opposing walls of the bathroom stalls. And mindful of her unwashed hands, Zora didn't put her arms around him, though she really, really wanted to.

"WEREN'T YOU SCARED?" she whispered, when later they were lying spoon-fashion and fully-clothed on her bed.

They had gone back and collapsed there, and had remained in that position for almost an hour, not speaking, but privately processing the strangely intimate experience.

"You kiddin' me?" Deuce said. "I was fucking terrified. I'm not ready to be anybody's daddy."

Zora laughed. "Okay. Because you made me kind of nervous you were so calm."

"I wasn't calm at all. If you looked and listened real close, I'm pretty sure you would've *seen* and heard my heart beating a million miles a minute."

Turning to face him, Zora was still smiling. "Well you didn't show it at all," she said.

"Because I knew *you* were scared. And I didn't want you to be."

"*Aww* ..." Zora felt a rush of unexpected tenderness for him. "*Babe.*"

He smiled at the endearment, but didn't remark on it. "I didn't want you to think it would be ... *tragic* or anything. I mean, we're not ready, either one of us ... and me and you, we're not there right now. But it wouldn't be tragic. Y'know?"

Zora nodded. She leaned in, softly pressing her lips to his.

"I was an 'oops' baby," he said unexpectedly. "My father wasn't much older than I am now, when I was born."

"How do you ... did they actually tell you that?" Zora asked. "That you were unplanned?"

"Not in so many words. But my whole life I've kind of known. I mean, my parents are ... let's just say there couldn't be two more incompatible people on the face of the earth."

Zora said nothing, wondering what it would have been like, to feel like you had been an accident; the rope that tethered together two people who would rather not have been.

For all her parents' issues, she had never felt that. She and her brother were the center of both their parents' lives. Her mother, who was an ER nurse, emailed her whenever young, Black men came in with gunshot wounds, or as a result of street violence. Though she didn't completely understand Zora's activism, she reached for every possible commonality in their respective worlds.

Her father was the same, though his tactic was different. He tried to interest Zora in Senegal, talking to her incessantly about the politics in his home country, seeking to make it as tantalizing as the social justice causes that so preoccupied her about the States. But with both her parents, Zora never lost the sense that she was like a jewel; something precious they never wanted to lose sight of, even though they were powerless over her growing independence.

"My mom got married a few years ago," Deuce continued. "To a dude who was a little younger than her. Just a few years younger. But he wanted kids, like bad. One time I heard them fighting and she told him she was never meant to be a mother. That I was the only kid she was ever going to have. They broke up not long after. I mean, they had other problems, but ... yeah, I think it was a wrap after that fight."

"Do you want a family one day?"

"Yeah," he said smiling at her like he'd only just realized it. "A big one, I think. One day."

THIRTEEN

"So, here's something you'd never guess about me," Zora said.

She was sitting cross-legged on his bed, and between them was a large platter of sushi, various kinds, because Deuce didn't know crap-all about sushi and each time he tried it, he wound up nauseated. But he'd gotten it for her, at great expense and inconvenience, because she was working on a paper and said she couldn't *possibly* go out, though it was a Friday night. But she had gone out – just to his room and just because he said he had something important he wanted to show her.

Having only vague ideas about how sushi-ordering worked, Deuce didn't realize that a "roll" was six pieces, so wound up getting enough, and in sufficient variety, that he could have fed four people. But Zora was jazzed at how enterprising he had been, to drive in the snow, to the only decent Japanese restaurant in town and bring her back the kind of food she rarely had the money and time to indulge in. When he opened the door to his room, and she saw the whole thing laid out, on a picnic blanket on his bed (because he had no other large surface that was clear) she literally squealed, jumping up and down and hugging him in her excitement.

Deprived of more intimate outlets, that's what they did now: they hugged. And he kissed her too, as often as he could, but Zora was always careful to cut those kisses short before they became too heated. Deuce still hadn't touched her. Not in the way he wanted to; not since New Year's Eve.

Though in all other ways they were openly a couple, the most intimate part of their relationship still hadn't resumed. He was dating her. *Dating.* He called her up and asked if she wanted to hang out; and if she wasn't out saving more Black lives, she would say yes.

And then he would stop by her room and they might go somewhere to eat; or watch a movie at his place since he had a state-of-the-art entertainment system. Occasionally, they just stayed in her room, doing not much of anything. If they went out and he came back with her, she generally showed him the door when it got late. Once, when he suggested that he could stay and they wouldn't do anything, Zora had straight up laughed at him.

Okay, sure, she said as she shut the door. *G'night.*

It was one thing if they were just getting to know each other, if there hadn't been all that ... *fucking* already. He knew every square-inch of Zora's body now—the tiny birthmark on her left inner-thigh, the dimples at the small of her back, the patch of lighter-toned skin under her right breast ... the fact that her second toes were slightly longer than her big toes ... He missed all of it.

Because of nights like the one they were having now, he felt both closer to her than he had ever been, and more estranged. Even the pregnancy scare had in some ways made them more solid. But he needed to feel her skin against his skin, and hear her soft, feathery breaths in his ear when she came, and have her arms and thighs locked tightly around him, trembling as she spent. Some days, the absence of a physical relationship with Zora felt to Deuce like a limb was missing.

"What would I never guess about you?" he asked.

"That I had nannies," Zora said, nodding as though pleased with the unexpected nature of her revelation. "Sometimes three at a time."

This did surprise him. Deuce's eyebrows lifted.

Zora grinned, and still nodding, reached down, and popped a tuna roll into her mouth. She had confessed to him that while she loved sushi, she was all-thumbs when it came to using chopsticks. The ones he'd brought along with the food had been tossed aside, unused.

"Want to know how come?" she asked.

"How come?" he asked, dutifully.

He was curious about the nannies, but distracted by the way she licked the soy sauce off her fingers, and by how long her legs looked in her black leggings.

"We went to Senegal when we were younger, my brother Ousmane and I. Sometimes for the entire summer. My father would bring us back to his village where he grew up, and they treated us like we were visiting royalty. All his sisters and brothers, cousins ... just this huge extended family.

"And they would all want to look after us, this little matched pair of African-yet-not-African babies. So, we always had nannies, but more than one. As if American babies require more care. Isn't that strange?"

Deuce shrugged. "American babies probably do require more care."

Zora tilted her head to one side as though she had never considered this. "Why?"

"We're the most pampered people on the face of the earth, Zee."

She shrugged and then ate another piece of sushi. "Maybe you're right. I've only ever been to Senegal and Mexico. How 'bout you?"

"I've been to a few places." He stretched out next to her, folding his arms beneath his head and looking up at the ceiling instead of at her. Her thigh was next to his cheek, so he had to fight the urge to turn his face toward it, and kiss it, and inhale her.

"Like ...?" she prompted.

"France, Germany, England. Italy, and for just one day, to Switzerland."

"Wow. But only Europe huh?"

"So far. Except one time to Mexico for Spring Break."

"I should take you to Senegal. It'd blow your mind."

"Yeah? Why?"

"You'll feel in touch with your Blackness there. And at the same time, you'll feel less than Black. Like some kind of ... hybrid."

"Is that how you felt?"

"Yeah." Zora's voice had grown a little distant, like she was remembering and re-experiencing something profound. "I felt ... dumb. And disconnected. And sometimes even ashamed."

"Why *ashamed*?" Deuce sat up again.

"Because I'm a mutt, by their standards, since I have an American mother. And I couldn't speak Wolof, which is the most commonly spoken native language. I couldn't even speak French. I felt ... I don't know ... ineffectual. I think that's why I stopped going. Around the time I was fifteen and my father let us decide whether we would go for the summer or not, I decided not to. Ousmane always wanted to go. And of course, now he speaks Wolof *and* French, but I still don't." Zora made a scoffing sound. "I was such an idiot."

Deuce stared at her for so long she blushed, and finally looked away.

"What?" she asked.

"You use words like 'ineffectual'. You think about things no other girl I know thinks about. Or talks about."

"Don't you ever think about things like that? What it means that you're here? And how, but for your parents making one slightly different choice, you wouldn't be who you are?"

"No," he said. "I don't think about stuff like that. Like, ever."

Zora seemed stunned by that admission. "You don't think ... for example, about how if your Dad never had the bravery to try to make it in an industry that was incredibly difficult to break into, you might have been the son of like, a music store clerk?"

Deuce reached over and shoved aside the platter of sushi— still way more than one person could eat—and tugged gently on the hem of Zora's cropped sweater. It stopped just above the waistband of her leggings, so he could see a tantalizing strip of incandescent, dark-brown skin. When he tugged, she scooted closer, still sitting cross-legged, but now directly facing him.

Reaching for one of the napkins, Deuce wiped her fingers clean of the sticky rice and soy sauce. Then, without thinking about it, without planning it, he put those fingers to his lips, kissed the tips of each one. The forefinger he pulled into his mouth and lightly sucked on the tip. It was salty from the soy sauce. When he saw Zora's deep swallow and her eyes darken, he leaned in and pressed his mouth against the side of her neck.

"I love how we talk," he said. "How we ... play ... how you ... make me think about shit I never thought about before. But I miss touching you, Zee. I miss ... us, how we are ... when we're together ..."

"I miss us too," she said. She sounded like she was having trouble catching her breath.

"Then ..."

"Sex is powerful. It can make you see things that aren't there. Or not see things that are ..."

"That's what I'm talkin' 'bout," Deuce said, his lips moved from her neck to her shoulder as he shoved the neckline of sweater further aside. "The things you *say* ... You need to ... quiet your mind sometimes."

"I just want to know that you see me. And that I see you. As we really are."

Hearing something in her voice that demanded focus, Deuce sat up. Zora's lips were slightly parted, the lower one moist. She would taste like sushi, but he didn't care.

"I see you," he said, with all the earnestness he could muster.

Zora studied him for a few moments then narrowed her eyes. "Are you *acting* right now?"

He grinned. "No. But I feel like I need to be really convincing so we can get past this and ... you know."

Zora spluttered into laughter then reached behind her and grabbed one of his pillows, hitting him over the head with it. Snatching it from her, he tossed it aside and with it, the remainder of Zora's sushi slid over the edge of the bed, and onto the floor.

"Oh crap! Look what you ..."

Deuce grabbed her by the waist and pulled her toward him, shifting their positions so she was on her back and he was poised above her.

"I don't care. We'll clean it up later."

"Tell me about the girls in Europe," Zora said, when he was just about to kiss her. "What were they like?"

He froze. "What makes you think I knew any girls in Europe?"

Zora gave him a look and he laughed. Still on top of her, he balanced the weight of his upper body on his elbows.

"Okay," he said. "Gimme a country ..."

"England."

"There was a girl named Pippa."

"Pippa," Zora repeated.

"Yeah, right? Who can take someone seriously whose name is Pippa?"

"Did you take *any* of them seriously?"

Her voice had changed. She was like other girls in this one way—they asked questions they knew the answer to, but they wanted to hear him say it, just so they could get themselves worked up.

"No. But that's not what's happening right here, with you and me." He nudged her knees further open and settled himself between them. He was already hard, and had to fight the impulse to move against her, to create friction.

"No?"

"No."

Her acquiescence was in the relaxation of her thighs, and in her eyes and in the way her lips parted slightly. But Deuce's first kiss was tentative. She tasted salty, and a little spicy. He made the kiss deeper and Zora's arms snaked around his neck.

This time, when he felt the urge to move, he did, creating pressure between them until he wasn't the only one moving. Zora's hips undulated beneath his and he eased up a little, just so he could concentrate on her movement and how good that felt. Her hair was out today, so he grasped it in his fists. It didn't matter how much of it he held in his hands, he could not contain it.

Pulling her head back to expose more of her neck, he kissed

her there, moving lower and then helping her remove her sweater. Beneath it, she was wearing only a delicate white bra. It was translucent and smooth. He looked at it and smiled, running his fingertips around the circle of her areolae until her nipples hardened. It unhooked in the front, so he undid it, and her breasts spilled out of the garment and apart.

"You're beautiful," he said, lowering his head to kiss one and then the other. He wanted to go slow this time, for her, and because it had been a long time. Relatively speaking.

"Wait," Zora said.

Deuce groaned and let his head fall back. "*Zee...*"

"No, silly. I just ... I want to try something."

"Something freaky?"

She laughed. "No. Not freaky. Just new. New for me, anyway." She shoved at his chest until he pulled back and was resting on his haunches, and then reached for the button-fly of his jeans.

"Wait a second," he said, putting his hand over hers. "You mean ..."

Zora nodded and licked her lower lip.

"So you never ..."

"Never."

"Like *never?*"

"Yes, Deuce, I mean never-never. You're making me feel like ... self-conscious about it now." She covered her face with her hands, and he pulled them away.

"Nah. Don't," he said, trying not to smile. *Fuck Rashad Dixon.* "Why me?" he asked.

"Because you're the guy who, when you thought I might be pregnant and ruin your entire life, you still wanted to make sure I wasn't scared."

"It wouldn't have ruined my life, Zora," he said shaking his head.

"But you would've been stuck with me—one way or another—for a very, *very* long time," she pointed out.

"That doesn't sound so bad." He kissed the side of her neck. "And anyway, you wouldn't have wanted to, you know, get rid of ..."

"No," she said, before he was even finished. "I think every woman has to make their own choice, but that's not a choice I could ever make."

Like the layers of an onion, they were peeling each other back, bit by bit. But even funnier was the fact that even what they were talking about right now didn't dampen the urge. Hell, he would wear two condoms if it made her feel better, but he was getting some tonight if it killed him.

"Get rid of those tights," Deuce said.

Zora peeled them off, and with it her underwear. She was completely naked now, and he was still fully-dressed.

"I could look at you all night," he said.

"I don't want you to look at me all night. I want you to touch me. And I want to touch you." She reached for the hem of his shirt and helped him pull it off. Then they removed the jeans and his boxer-briefs. When he was as naked as she was, she stared at him. Just her staring brought him back to full arousal. And then she took a deep breath and slowly lowered her head.

"Hey." He touched her shoulder. "You don't have to ..."

"Quiet," she said, like someone who was concentrating on a particularly confounding problem and been interrupted.

And when her lips finally closed over him, Deuce wasn't sure which was better—the sight of them, plush and plum-hued, or the velvety smooth sensation of being in her mouth. Sighing, he closed his eyes.

"No." Zora pulled back for a moment. "I want you to watch me," she said.

DEUCE STEPPED into sushi when he got off the bed. The slimy fish and soft rice squished between his toes and he cursed quietly, trying not to wake Zora who was still lying facedown in the covers, hugging the pillow with both arms.

Using paper from his printer, he scooped the remains of her dinner off the floor and dumped it all into his trashcan, then tied it off to take with him to the bathroom down the hall. Because who wanted to wake up to the smell of day-old uncooked fish?

Dragging on his briefs, he shoved open the door and stumbled out into the hallway. He needed to go. And bad. He needed to go badly an hour ago, but Zora was asleep on top of him and he didn't want to risk waking her. Now that she had rolled off him all on her own, he was free, finally, to go relieve his bladder.

On the way down the hall, he encountered a drunk couple, and a few guys sitting on the floor outside a room they were apparently locked out of. Slurring their words and passing a bottle in a paper sack between them, they were loudly debating whether the word "genius" was a fair assessment of David Bowie, or whether the label was only now being applied because he was dead.

"He was a genius," Deuce opined, as he walked by, carrying his plastic bag of ruined sushi.

"*Thank* you!" one of the guys yelled throwing both arms up in the air like someone indicating a touchdown.

He took a leak and washed his hands, looking at his reflection in the mirror. Right about now, on a Friday night, he would normally be at a party, scanning the room, wondering whether there was anyone interesting enough to talk to, to make a move on, to take home. But instead, here he was.

"Here I am," he said aloud to his reflection. Thinking about what awaited him, back in his room, he gave his reflection a wide, smug grin.

He was halfway back down the hall when he realized what he was looking at: Zora at the door to his dorm room, with the sheet wrapped around her; and standing at the threshold, Caroline Farber.

Fuck.

Forcing himself not to break into a run, Deuce nevertheless picked up the pace. But by the time he got there, Caroline was turning to go, and only spared him the briefest of glances before she hurried down the hall, her platinum-blonde ponytail bouncing and swinging behind her. She looked back just once. Her face was bright-red and she was biting into her lower lip. Zora stood in the doorway and offered him one hard and lethal look, then turned on her heel and went back inside.

He shut the door and studied her face as she sat on the edge of his bed.

"Sorry I opened your door," she said, her voice flat. "When I heard the knocking, and saw you weren't next to me, I thought maybe you went to the bathroom and locked yourself out."

"You don't have to apologize for that, Zee. You're my girl, so ..."

"And that girl? Who ... when was ..."

"Before you. A while before."

Zora considered this for a moment, and Deuce watched her consider it. Finally, she seemed to decide to believe him, and lay on her side, her back facing him. She pulled the sheet up over her shoulders. He reached out, but was reluctant to touch her, because he could see the tension in her shoulders.

"What did you say to her?" he asked when the room was dark again.

"I told her ..." Zora began speaking and her voice was still tight with anger. "That you're not interested in her anymore, that you're with me now. And that if she has any sense of pride whatsoever she won't ever come back here."

In the dark, Deuce grinned.

"I didn't like doing that. And I shouldn't have to," Zora said. "Make sure it never happens again."

FOURTEEN

Zora tried to focus.

Next to her, Rashad had just finished with his rallying cry and when the cheering reached a crescendo, lifted his arms above his head in the 'Hands Up' gesture that had become symbolic of their movement. Their audience followed suit, and after a few moments of silence for lives lost, the rally was over.

The rally was over.

And Deuce hadn't come.

"Our numbers are low," Rashad said leaning over and speaking into her ear. "The room wasn't even full."

"Because we're not asking them to do anything," Amira chimed in.

Amira, who had been one of the most active members of the chapter since it began, was a beautiful sister with long, auburn locs. Lately, Zora noticed, she had begun to materialize more often than before, at Rashad's side. Especially when, as now, he initiated a private conversation with Zora.

"You can only ask people to come out to express their outrage so many times before they lose interest," Amira continued. "We need to think of something that's going to have impact. So they feel the empowerment."

Rashad shrugged and looked at Zora. "She's right."

"Yeah, she is." Zora nodded. Then, realizing that she was talking about Amira as though she wasn't even there, she faced her and nodded again. "You're right. We're losing steam."

"Let's go grab some coffee and talk about it," Rashad suggested. "You got time?"

Glancing once again out into the dwindling crowd, she made a sound of assent, and followed Rashad and Amira out of the hall.

They chose a place just off campus where the coffee was terrible, but the apple pie a la mode was some of the best in the state. The portion sizes were monstrous, and had scored them a spot on *Diners Drive Ins and Dives* on the Food Network. Since then, a place that used to be a little-known local haunt had become a genuine local attraction. But Penn State students, recognized by the proprietor never had to wait for a booth and tonight was no different. As soon as they walked in, Zora, Rashad and Amira were shown to their table.

Waving away menus, they all ordered from memory. Moments after they sat, Amira excused herself to go to the ladies' room. Zora and Rashad stared at each other for a few moments until she cleared her throat.

"You and Amira then, huh?"

He lifted his brows. "What makes you say ...?"

"I can read your body language like a book, Shad. And the way she just slid in right next to you just now, staking out her claim ..." Her voice sounded bitter.

"I like her." Rashad shrugged. "She's on point with ..."

"She the kind of woman you see as your ... destiny?" Zora asked.

Shaking his head, he gave a brief laugh. "C'mon, Zora. You get to move on but I don't?"

"Of course you do," she said fidgeting with her paper napkin. "It's just that every time I speak more than two words to you lately, she's there, like a ... guard dog. Or a puppy."

Rashad gave her a look.

"Okay, fine. That was uncalled for. But it's annoying the way she just buzzes around and tries to take over."

"She admires you," Rashad said matter-of-factly. "Looks up to you. It would be a real shame if you couldn't return that admiration with something like ... common decency."

Zora looked down at her lap, feeling a tiny twinge of shame. Shad had always been able to appeal to her better angels.

"I don't know what's going to happen with me and her." He shrugged. "Probably not much. I'm leaving for Stanford in the fall, so I'm not tryin' to start nothin' serious right now, anyway. Not that it should matter to you anymore."

"You're always going to matter to me."

"Zora. What's really going on? Because I know this ain't about me."

She looked away. He was right. She didn't care about who Shad was grooming to be his new "destiny." It was about Deuce not being at the rally. And about him not being there for Black Caucus meetings, or showing anything akin to genuine interest when she talked about her work. It was about the fact that despite his lack of interest, she still wanted him like she had never wanted anyone before.

And if it was just ... wanting, then it might have been easier to stomach. But it was much more than that. Lately, their sex had tapered off a little. But in the best way. For a while once it resumed, there was something almost grasping and desperate about their sex life; the way they *had to* have each other, as often as four times a week.

Now, they had settled in a rhythm that felt more secure and Zora noticed the subtleties, the kinds of things that made relationships last, maybe even for a long, long, time. His mellow energy balanced her frenetic nature. His humor helped her not take herself so seriously. His unexpectedly sweet and romantic nature made her less of a cynic. And she was just plain ol' happier when he was around. They even had their *own* epic-ass conversations. Not the same as those she'd had with Rashad, but that didn't matter because Deuce was *not* Shad, nor would she want him to be.

But still, Deuce's interest in her work was that of a bystander. Whatever epiphanies he had when they met were once again trumped by hanging out with Kal, and that large group of knuckleheaded athletes whose only interest seemed to be 'scoring' as many women as they could before graduation.

"No, I'm just … distracted," Zora lied. "Stressed about declaring a major … trying to figure out my life."

Rashad put a hand on the table and slid it across toward hers until their fingertips touched. "You can call me, y'know? Always."

"I know I can. But should I?" Zora put her hand over his. "I'm pretty sure that wouldn't be healthy for either of our relationships."

Just as Shad was about to respond, Amira was back. Seeing their hands joined on the table, she paused for a nanosecond before sitting and forcing a smile.

"So," she said brightly, as Rashad and Zora pulled apart. "Should we talk strategy?"

———

IT WAS after midnight when the pounding on her door awakened Zora from what wasn't a very deep slumber to begin with.

Opening it, she stepped aside for Deuce who came in, bringing a boozy cloud with him. When she shut the door, he pressed her against it and kissed her, his mouth tasting like rum, mixed with something bittersweet. Zora submitted to the kiss for a few moments then shoved him away.

"What have you been ...?"

"Baby, you're never going to believe ..."

"Where the hell were you?" she snapped.

He looked confused for a minute then grimaced. "Shit. The rally. How'd that go?"

"It went," she said tightly. Folding her arms, she went to sit on the edge of her bed.

"So you want to hear about my night, or no?" he asked.

Deuce shrugged his sweatshirt over his head, leaving only a plain white t-shirt. When she didn't answer, he shrugged and kept talking.

"Guess who drove up to see me."

Zora said nothing.

"Jamal Turner."

Still, she said nothing.

"Okay, so you don't get it. Lemme explain it to you. I sent him a business plan a couple weeks ago. Y'know what you said about earning my father's respect? I've been thinking about that, workin' on it, y'know what I mean? So I wrote up this plan about this new label, how we'd use the college circuit to iden-tify and groom new talent. Like real-deal talent. Labels don't do that no more. They just crank out insta-stars through social media, sometimes folks who haven't even been really tested with live audiences too much.

"So my plan would take us back to the basics. That's how The Fugees started, doin' college tours and shit like that. Anyway, Jamal read it, and liked it. And he came up here to talk to me about it. Just showed up out of nowhere. He acted like he had business in town, but who the fuck has music-related business in State College, Pennsylvania, right?"

Despite herself, Zora felt her interest pique a little. "Couldn't he have just sent someone?" she asked; but grudgingly, because she wasn't sure she wanted Deuce to know she was interested. "Like, isn't he the head guy, of like, the whole company?"

"Yes! Exactly! That's how I know it's big. Because he came to talk to me when he could have sent someone or shit, he could've Facetimed me or something. But he came and said he wanted to take me out to dinner to talk about it."

"But he's also a good friend of your father's so ..."

"So you're sayin' you think he threw me a bone. Because I'm my father's son."

Zora shrugged. "No. I don't know. Just that, he probably would have sent someone if you were just some kid who ..."

Deuce's face fell and he collapsed on her bed next to her, lying on his back and looking at the ceiling instead of at her. "He probably wouldn't have even read the proposal if I was just some anonymous college kid. Yeah, I know that. But thanks for reminding me. My point is, he didn't have to come, and he did. And he liked the plan. Anyway ... we're going to work on it together. And I'll have a job with him this summer."

But now he looked deflated, and Zora felt ashamed. She touched his knee.

"That's great. I just ... I wanted you at the rally, that's all."

Deuce exhaled heavily. "*You* wanted."

"Yes! But only because you said you would come! So don't blame me for being disappointed that you didn't show. And didn't text .... The room wasn't even half full so it would have been nice to have the support."

"How about you show *me* some support? I just told you that something I only dreamed about, something I never thought could happen, might happen. That I might get a chance to start this label from the ground up with ..."

Zora sighed.

"Yeah, I know. This shit is boring to you. Meaningless. *Shallow*. And the only people who do important work, are you and those Hotep muthafuckas you hang out with. The rest of us are just ... *lost* and shit.

"But this is what I want to do with my life. *Music*. So excuse me if I didn't stop in the middle of my business conversation with the head of Scaife Enterprises to text my girlfriend that I couldn't make it to her little rally when two hundred *other* muthafuckas would be there!"

"There weren't two hundred," Zora said evenly. "Barely even eighty. That's the point. If there were only two people in the room, Deuce, I would want you to be one of them!"

"Oh, so I have to be your cheering section, but you don't have to be mine? Why? Because my cause isn't worthy enough? Y'know what ..." He shoved himself up again and reached for his sweatshirt. "Fuck this shit. Because your ass ain't never fuckin' happy. Doesn't matter what the hell I do!"

"And what *do* you do? Besides yuck it up with Kal and those ...."

"Shut up about Kal. He has nothing but good things to say about you."

"And you have good things to say about my crew? Those 'Hotep muthafuckas' I think you called them?"

"It's one thing to be Black and woke, Zora. It's another thing to look down on other Black folks because their priorities are different than yours. And that's what you do ... you even look down on me ..."

"I don't look down on you. I just want ... more for you."

"I don't need you to want anything for me. I know what I want for myself. And if it's too different from what you want ...

if it's not ... *noble* enough, maybe we need to just call this shit a day and ... go our separate ways."

Zora felt her eyes fill. She said nothing, but stared at Deuce who was staring back just as hard at her. His eyes were red. She couldn't tell whether it was from emotion or the drinking he'd been doing earlier.

"We're *fuckin' twenty-years old*, Zee. It's not a crime to want to do something besides save the damn world. I bend over *backwards* to make your ass happy. I do shit I never fuckin' did ... *never fuckin' did* for any chick. Just to make you happy. And you just ... always want to be mad at some shit."

Blinking repeatedly to stop the tears from falling, Zora stood and shook her head.

"Then don't do it anymore," she said going to the door and opening it. "Don't bend over backwards, Deuce."

"Zee ..."

"G'night," she said, holding the door wider.

"Zee ..."

"Get out of my room."

"No. Zee ..."

"Get out of my room!"

Deuce reached over and shoved the door shut. "No," he said, the quiet of his voice in contrast to her loudness. His eyes were filling too. He took a step toward her and she took one back. He extended a hand. "C'mere."

Zora hesitated, her chest heaving from the effort it took not to cry.

"I didn't mean it," he said, his throat bobbing. "I don't want to go our separate ways. I don't ... I would never want that."

Zora stood, frozen in place and then unexpectedly, Deuce came toward her, lifting her bodily and carrying her toward the bed. Placing her atop the covers, he pulled her underwear unceremoniously down over her hips and fell to his knees in front of her.

"Deuce," she said weakly, her hand on his head.

"I don't want to fight, baby ..." he said. "I'm sorry. I just want ... I want to make you feel good ... okay? Let's just ..."

"But we have to ..."

His tongue touched her, and the last word came out in a squeak: *talk.*

We need to talk.

That's what she meant to say, but didn't, because the sensation of Deuce's mouth and tongue, and the hungry way he was going at her drove almost all coherent thought from her head. He pressed her thighs apart with his forearms and at the same time gripped her waist, holding her against the sheets while he tasted her.

When she cried out, it sounded like agony as much as it did pleasure, and the tears she had been holding at bay were released in a flood. While she lay there, tears streaming down the side of her face, Deuce undressed, and covered her body with his. Zora felt him fumbling for a moment, finding and putting on a condom, and then he was surging forward and pushing deep into her.

He filled her with the very first thrust, and she gripped his butt, pulling him closer still. She arched off the bed, pushing upward with every downward motion, feeling the muscles in his haunches tense and release. He seemed to want to bury his entire body inside her. Zora moved between total awareness of every tiny frisson of pleasure, and an almost dissociative state where she was watching them together rather than being present in her own body. Because the pleasure was at times too much.

Closing her eyes, she felt his face buried in her neck, heard him speaking words that were unintelligible, directly into her ear. Then in what seemed like a frenzy, he grabbed her chin and forced her head toward him, capturing her mouth and kissing her hard, demanding her attention. Dissociation was impossible then. She held on tight, riding the waves to her second orgasm, and her body went limp beneath him. Deuce slowed, kissing her now perspiring forehead, his strokes slow and gentle until finally he, too, shuddered and was still.

Lifting a hand, Zora placed it on his damp cheek. Turning her head, she placed her lips against his neck, tasting his saltiness.

"I'm sorry, too," she whispered.

Deuce put his arms beneath her and rolled over, carrying her with him so she was now lying atop his damp chest.

"It's okay, baby," he said, his voice already clogged with exhaustion. His arms tightened about her. "We're good. It's all good."

But it wasn't. She knew it, and suspected he did, too.

It wasn't all good.

FIFTEEN

The bass was pounding in his chest, and the room was an unpleasant mass of bodies, moist and warm from heavy coats and the recent snowfall outside. Deuce pushed his way toward the makeshift bar and grabbed one of the cups of beer that had been set down on the table, up for grabs for whomever got there first. The music was so loud that the lyrics were incomprehensible, and it was only by concentrating that he recognized the artist. It was Devin Parks.

Lately, he had been hitting his stride, and Deuce guessed that it would only be six to nine months before he was a bonafide star. That would be something to see. Deuce wondered who was working with him, and whether he was being cooperative. It would be a shame to see him mishandled, because he was one of the types of musicians that Deuce had talked to Zora about—a true artist. Too bad he had heartthrob appeal, because it was going to be difficult for his label to resist trying to turn him into a pop idol.

Leaning against a nearby wall, Deuce sighed and scanned

the room. No sign of Zora. She'd promised to meet him here after her Black Caucus subcommittee meeting, but by his watch, that should have ended an hour ago. And still no sign of her. But it had become par for the course with them lately. Like ships passing in the proverbial night.

Ever since they fought about him missing her rally, they seemed to have agreed, silently, not to fight anymore. So, they didn't. They just went their separate ways, pursuing their separate interests, with their separate friends; and coming together only when they were alone, or spending the night at each other's place. That should have been the hallmark of a healthy relationship—pursuing independent lives—but something about it didn't feel right. It didn't feel like they were accommodating their differences, but avoiding them.

Nearby, Kal had some chick cornered, literally. She was at the edge of the room and Kaleem stood in front of her, leaning forward, his forearm braced on the wall above her head.

Deuce smirked. Ol' girl didn't stand a chance.

Kal laughed at something and when he shifted a little to the left, Deuce saw that his prey for the evening was Zora's girl Mia.

Gulping down the last of the lukewarm beer in his cup, he headed in their direction.

"Hey," he said, speaking loudly enough to be heard over the music. "Mia. What's up?"

She looked away from Kal reluctantly and then smiled when she saw it was him.

"Oh hey!" she said.

"Know where Zee is at?" Deuce asked.

Mia shrugged. "Still at the meeting? I don't know. A couple of them were talking about celebrating when I left, so ..."

"Celebrating what?"

"The article finally came out. The Pittsburgh Post-Gazette ran it. They thought it was only going to be local, but yeah ... it got picked up elsewhere."

Deuce narrowed his eyes in confusion.

"The one on BLM," Mia explained. "Zora didn't tell you? My girl's a genuine regional superstar now."

Rather that admit he didn't know what she was talking about, Deuce nodded and shoved his way outside, finding and shrugging on his coat as he went. Once on the curb, he blew into his palms to warm them up and texted Zora, asking if she was still on her way.

Yup, she responded. *Be there in five minutes.*

I'm outside, he texted back. *Look for me.*

And sure enough, no more than a few minutes later, a familiar car pulled up and Zora hopped out, smiling, and waving at the driver as it pulled away. She was wearing a large knit hat that contained her massive hair, and a red, yellow, green and black scarf that looped several times around her neck and covered the lower part of her face. Making her way precariously in the snow, she leaned against him when they were finally face-to-face.

"My hands are freezing," she sang. "Otherwise I would hug you."

Instead, she got up on her toes and kissed him on the lips. She tasted of beer, and, unless Deuce was mistaken, weed as well. He didn't kiss her back. But Zora didn't seem to notice. She hopped up and down a little and nudged him in the direction of the party.

"Are we going in?"

Almost no one else was outside, because it was far too cold for folks to hang about on the porch the way they customarily might have done.

"You sure you want to?" he asked. "Seems like you already did some partying tonight."

Zora laughed, oblivious to the light sarcasm. "Yeah, a few of us went back to Shad's for a minute. Today was kind of a big day."

"Yeah? Tell me about it." Deuce shoved his hands deep into his pockets, thinking about the mysterious article that Mia had referred to.

"Out here?" Zora looked around. "How 'bout we go in, see what's up with this party and then talk about it later?"

"For a minute," he capitulated.

"Remember, this party was your idea," she said, again in the sing-song voice that meant she had probably taken a few more puffs on the spliff than he first guessed at.

Looping her arm through his, Zora walked with him up the path and they headed inside.

Whenever they entered a room together now, it was like a figurative parting of the Red Sea. People turned to stare at them, the unlikely couple. Deuce knew it was only partly a function of their being independently notorious for very different reasons. The other part was that people weren't used to seeing him so comfortably coupled up. He went to lots of parties with lots of girls. Or used to.

But they were always in his orbit more than they were "with" him. With those girls, he walked into a room the way he always did; and it was they who hovered, angling and leaning their bodies toward his, making sure everyone knew that they were with him, but never daring to do anything so overt as hold his hand.

With Zora, it was different. He held her hand, always. Or she tucked herself under his arm and pulled it across her chest. They were unmistakably a couple and most often, he was the one doing the claiming; he was the one who was possessive of her.

"Whoa," Zora said, taking a step back. The mild stench of the room hit them like a noxious cloud as soon as they walked in the door. "Yeah, this is going to be quick."

But then she spotted Mia, in the middle of the crowd dancing with Kal and they both let out those high-pitched screams that girls greeted each other with when they were excited for reasons only known to them. Zora and Mia ran toward each other, hugging and dancing in the center of the floor while Kal and Deuce exchanged perplexed and amused looks.

Kal ambled over to him and without a word, pulled out his phone tapping its face and handing it to him.

"Check this out," he said. "I guess this is what all the screaming is about."

It was a page from the Post-Gazette, with the headline: 'A Human Rights Issue.' The piece seemed to be a lengthy one, so Deuce only caught a few phrases as he scrolled through: 'local activist, Rashad Dixon, affectionately called Shad by his chapter co-chair and girlfriend Zora Diallo' and 'seemed politically and tactically in sync, often finishing each other's sentences and looking to the other for confirmation of ideas expressed' and 'dynamic partnership that, if indicative of the caliber of their leadership, augers well for Black Lives Matter as a sustainable social justice movement.'

But if that weren't enough, there were the pictures. Deuce magnified each one to get the full effect.

In the first, Rashad Dixon sat with his elbows on his knees, one hand stroking his bootleg Malcolm X goatee, looking pensively at Zora who was next to him, and gesturing, her mouth partly open as though the photographer had caught her mid-sentence. Her hair was resplendent, and her skin glowed. She was wearing lipstick, which she rarely did, and a black turtleneck sweater and black jeans. Her limbs were long, and graceful like those of a prima ballerina, one long leg crossed over the other. Sitting very close together, their knees almost touching, she and Rashad had the posture of two people accustomed to being in each other's space, and comfortable with it.

In the second shot, clearly taken during a lull in the interview, Zora and Rashad were almost huddled, both of them leaning in to the other, their eyes fixed on each other's faces. Zora was making a funny face, her small, cute nose wrinkled. Rashad was grinning at her, his teeth pulling in his lower lip as though to prevent himself from smiling any wider, or laughing. That shot was the one that made Deuce's blood boil, for reasons he couldn't even explain. They weren't even touching, and yet they were the very picture of intimacy.

Handing Kal the phone he glanced out at the dance-floor where Zora was still lost in the music, holding both Mia's hands, singing along to the lyrics. Just as he made up his mind to go get her, Deuce watched Zora and Mia stumble over toward the bar, both of them grabbing cups of the crappy, warm beer and tossing them back like they might shots of tequila.

Next to him, Kal laughed. "Mia is nice, don't get me wrong, but I still feel some type of way 'bout how you just moved in and ..."

"You read the article?" Deuce asked.

Kal looked at him. "Who's got time to read the news at a party, bruh? I just asked Mia what she was talkin' 'bout and she showed it to me. Your girl looks righteous in those pictures, though."

His girl. Not according to the article.

After their drinks, Zora and Mia made their way back out onto the dance floor, spinning and twirling and bopping off-

beat. Deuce, for a moment was too preoccupied with his irritation to see what he should have seen the moment she arrived.
Zora had no business being at anyone's party; a couple more
drinks and she would be straight up wasted. Wading through
the dancers, Deuce finally got to her and she looked up at him,
genuine surprise, and delight in her eyes, as though she had no
idea how he'd gotten there.

Momentarily forgetting his annoyance, Deuce grinned and
let her hug him, but Zora had other ideas in mind. She was
actually trying to *climb* him. Yeah, forget two more drinks; she
was wasted now. Grabbing her by the butt, he hoisted her up
and Zora immediately wrapped her legs around his hips, her
arms locked tightly around his neck.

"I want to go home now," she said against his ear, like a
little kid pleading to be carried up to bed. "It *stinks* in here.
Can you take me home?"

"Yeah," he said, more to himself than to her. "I'll take you
home."

ZORA SHOT UPRIGHT, arms flailing, almost slamming
Deuce in the side of the head as she did. Looking wildly
around, her eyes finally came to rest on his face and her shoulders relaxed. She fell backward onto the bed again and exhaled.

"Oh," she groaned. "I didn't know where I was for a
second."

"You remember anything from last night?" he asked
impassively.

Deuce hadn't slept well. When he got Zora back to his
room, he'd carefully undressed her while she babbled on, saying
over and over: *Deuce, I did* not *drink responsibly tonight, did I?*
No, I didn't. I did not *drink responsibly.*

After pulling a t-shirt over her head and putting her under the covers, he fired up his laptop and read the piece in the Post-Gazette. It was a good article. Some might even say it was a triumph. It made Zora and Rashad's BLM chapter and its work seem almost mainstream, but in a good way.

Rashad came across as level-headed and articulate, and Zora came across as what she was—a young woman in some ways mature beyond her years, with a clear and long vision for her future and that of the people she was working for. She didn't even sound like someone Deuce would know, let alone someone who would be in his bed, sleeping off a bender in his t-shirt, so big on her it gaped at the neck.

After reading it (twice) he sat up for a few hours more, staring out at the snow-filled yard just outside his window. It was almost dawn before he could even think about sleep. When he got into bed next to Zora, she burrowed into his side and made a sound like a purr that made him smile. Her hair smelled smoky and coconutty. He brushed his cheeks against its coarseness and tried to drive from his mind the premonition that it might be the last time they would lay together like this.

Now, looking at him with still-sleepy eyes, Zora smiled. "I don't remember a thing. Actually ... scratch that. I remember *some* things."

"The article."

Zora beamed. "Yes! You saw it?"

Deuce nodded. "It's going to be huge for you."

"For *me*?" Zora sat up again. "For the chapter. For the *movement*. It'll be one of the first times BLM gets written about as other than some radical, anti-American, subversive, group of racial separatists. Who cares about *me*?"

"I do," he said.

Zora looked quizzical for a moment then cocked her head to one side. "Are you talking about the ...?"

"The part where he referred to you as Rashad's girlfriend, his partner. Yeah. That didn't feel too good to read."

Her shoulders sagged. "Everyone who knows me, who knows Shad, knows that's not accurate. And you know I would have corrected it if ..."

Deuce shook his head. "Don't."

"*Babe* ..."

"It wasn't just that. I read the whole thing, and y'know what? Reading how you talked about the movement, how he talked about it ... I think I got it. For the first time, I got it."

"Got what?" Zora asked. She looked fearful.

"Why it is you get so impatient with me. And with everyone who isn't onboard."

"I never said you weren't onboard, Deuce. Just that I need your support. Or sometimes just your ... presence."

"I'm here, Zee. I've always been here with you. Even when you're not here with me."

"What does *that* mean?"

"You're on some next level shit ... and I'm ..."

"Don't tell me you're intimidated by a little press. You've been in the press practically your entire life."

She was trying to lighten things up. Probably because she read in his eyes some hint of the conviction that had just struck him that morning like an iron mallet in the center of his chest—Zora Diallo was going places. Places that maybe he didn't even yet understand. She looked right in that picture with Rashad Dixon because maybe it *was* right.

"I'm holding you back, maybe."

"How?" Zora grabbed his arm. "What are you *talking* about? You've never stopped me from doing anything I needed to do. And you make it so easy for me to ..."

"That's not what you said last week, Zee. When I wasn't at that rally ..."

"Babe, I was trippin'. I just … we'd had that weird thing with that girl showing up at your room and I was feeling inse-cure … and of course I just like having you there. But if I knew you were having a big night as well, I never would've expected …"

She was babbling a mile a minute now, struggling to convince him that everything was cool. But it didn't feel cool. It felt completely out of whack. His girl was looking to save Black bodies from bullets, and he was looking to discover the next Meshell Ndegeocello.

In the middle of one of her run-on sentences, her phone chimed and Zora looked around, annoyed, finally finding it on the desk where Deuce had placed it the night before. Looking at the screen, she did a double-take.

"I have no idea who this is, from a 212 area-code."

"Go ahead," Deuce said getting up from his spot on the bed. "Answer it."

She did, having a conversation with someone that was surprisingly easy to read, even hearing only one side. When she hung up, she looked thunderstruck.

"That was a producer in New York. From CNN. They want to interview me and Shad. She said she already talked to him, and he's into it, but wanted to have her ask me directly."

Deuce nodded. He heard enough to know it was a reporter, but CNN?

"Damn," he said, coming back to sit next to her.

She nodded dumbly.

"You can't pass that up," he said. "You have to do it."

"I have to do it," she agreed.

"When is it?"

"They want us to fly out tonight. We'd be on the morning show, the one with the governor's brother …They're going to have tickets at the airport waiting for us, and …"

Deuce kept his expression stoic though his stomach was in knots. He knew it would happen. But he was unprepared for just how quick it would be.

Last night, staring out at the snowy yard, he finally realized that it was only a matter of time before the competing demands of their respective lives pulled them apart. He just would never have believed it to be the very next day.

But he knew how these things worked. After CNN, everyone was going to jump on the bandwagon. They would be hearing from news outlets all over the country, looking to put their own unique spin on it. Who could resist the story that had been written in the Post-Gazette, of young lovers, out to change the world? And if they traveled the country, living the part, soon Rashad and Zora wouldn't be able to resist it either. And it would become true once again.

"You've got a lot to do, then," he forced himself to say. "If you leave tonight."

"Yeah, but babe ... what we were talking about before ..."

"When you get back," he said. "You should probably prepare, right? Do your talking points and all that?"

"Yeah, I should probably connect with Shad and come up with a game-plan."

"Okay, so get dressed. I'll walk you back to your dorm."

Zora licked her lower lip and looked conflicted, but eventually nodded and got up from the bed. Deuce looked away while she dressed, and stood to do the same.

The walk back to her dorm was a silent one, both of them trudging through the snow, Zora holding on to his arm at points to maintain her balance. The steady pressure of her small hands seemed to penetrate the layers of his coat and the shirts beneath. He'd always liked the way she did that—held onto him, tight, like she didn't want him to get away. She was a cool chick, and didn't often let it all hang out there, but there was no mistaking the meaning of the way she held him when they were out: *I am his, and he is mine.* He didn't often think about how good that felt, because he'd always been so busy holding on to her himself.

But perhaps, now, it was time to let go.

SIXTEEN

"You're making me nervous, Zora. Are you even listening to me?" The strain and impatience were clear in Rashad's voice.

"Yes, I'm listening! But you're making *me* nervous. We can't rehearse everything we say, Shad. Or it's going to come across as fake."

"I'm not concerned about it being fake. I don't doubt that you'll mean every word you say, just that you'll freeze up when asked a question and forget *which* words to say."

"Great. Go ahead and put *that* out there," Zora snapped.

They were in his apartment, and the clock was not Zora's friend. Their flight was leaving in four hours, and she had hoped to get back to campus with enough time to have Deuce come over so they could talk. If that phone call hadn't interrupted them, she knew he was about to break up with her. Maybe he didn't even know it, but she heard it, the air of finality and resignation in his voice, the imminent separation.

When that stupid interview happened, she knew she should have had Rashad correct the reporter's impression that they were together. And now, not only was it messing with her relationship, it was going to become national folklore. How the hell were they supposed to screw with that little fantasy? Especially now that it had become one of the hooks that would get BLM exactly the kind of positive national story they had been fruitlessly trying to orchestrate for months.

"Look. Are you packed already?" Rashad stood and paced his living room. "Because we ain't gettin' nowhere right now."

"Exactly what I've been saying. Thank you." Zora stood and grabbed her backpack.

Amira, sitting on the sofa, was watching the exchange between her and Rashad, almost ashen-faced. She had never heard them argue before. Probably because Zora and Rashad never had argued before, she realized. *Never*. How was that possible, in a two-year relationship?

She and Deuce seemed to be arguing all the time. Even before the newspaper piece came out, there had been fits-and-starts while they tried to figure each other out. But at no point had she been willing to throw in the towel. So why was he? She needed to talk to him, but this thing, this trip was standing in the way of that. She was surprised to resent the obligation, for that reason alone—it was standing in the way of her getting to Deuce, and working things out.

"Do you even want to do this?" Rashad demanded, as though he'd read her mind.

"Of course, I want to do it," Zora spat, shrugging on her coat. "It's what we've been working for, isn't it?"

"Because ..." He shook his head. "This is supposed to be a triumph. And you're acting like it's a fuckin' chore."

"Guys," Amira said, standing, and holding up both her hands. "The energy in here is taking a turn for the worse, so let's just remember what this is all about, okay?"

Zora exhaled through her nostrils. "I don't know. Maybe you should do it, Amira. I mean ..."

"Me?" she squeaked.

"Her?" Rashad said at the exact same time. "They didn't ask for her. They want you."

"They want the story you sold—of you and me like a social justice Bonnie and Clyde ..."

"That's a terrible analogy," Amira laughed.

"Whatever! You know what I mean!" Zora screamed.

Both Amira and Rashad stood very still, exchanging looks, taken aback at her outburst.

"Amira," Rashad said. "You want to give me and Zora a minute?"

Without another word, Amira disappeared in the direction of the kitchen, and Shad motioned for Zora to come closer. When she did, he pulled her into a hug. For a second, she resisted, but he held her fast.

"Breathe," he said. "Just breathe."

"Shad ..."

"*Breathe*," he insisted. He inhaled and Zora inhaled with him. Their chests pressed together as they exhaled in sync. Then he held her at arms' length, looking into her eyes. Zora stared back and when he smiled, his eyes were warm and full of love, hers filled with tears.

"Is this what you want?" he asked her. "Because after this, maybe it gets bigger. Bigger than either of us."

"I don't know," Zora admitted. "I mean, you know I'm committed ..."

"I know," Shad said nodding.

"... but I haven't even decided what I want to do with my life yet, and it feels like a life is choosing me rather than the other way around, and ..."

"I know," he said again. Then he shrugged. "And sometimes that's how it happens. I mean, until I lost someone, personally, I don't know that I would have made this choice either. But eventually, I did choose. And you should too. *You* decide. And if you decide to get off this train right now, I support you one hundred percent. This is my life's work now. It doesn't have to be yours."

"But the interview ..."

"I'd go in there and handle it. Don't worry about it."

"You *would* handle it, wouldn't you?" Zora said with a tiny smile. "I don't doubt that for a second."

"You know me, baby," Shad said winking at her. "So go on back to the dorms and pack. Or don't pack. I'll swing by on the way to the airport, and you get in the car with me. Or not. But either way, we'll be cool."

"You wouldn't hate me for bailing on you at the most critical of critical moments?"

Shad pulled her into a hug again, speaking into her hair. "What'd I tell you about that? I could never hate you, Zora. *Never.*"

GLANCING AT HER PHONE, Zora checked the time. Shad said he would text when he was outside, and didn't ask whether she was leaning one way or another. Because he was patient that way.

But if he was worried, he needn't be. Because Zora was going. She had to.

It wasn't just about her, and her career aspirations. Probably hundreds of thousands of people would be watching that CNN segment, and what they saw could shape the narrative for the movement for months to come. And even if that was an overstatement, it would certainly set the tone for the next few weeks, and give them time to regroup. So, of course she would go. She would go, and she would put on the performance of her life, being everything America needed her to be, so they could understand ...

"Get over yourself, Zora," she whispered.

The thing of it was, she was just a momentary symbol. There were others like her. Hundreds who could sit in her place, and who would. Amira for one. But for this moment in time, it was her and she would play her part.

And afterwards, she would come back and get her man.

She wasn't quitting the movement, or the Black Caucus. It didn't have to be as stark a choice as all that. But Deuce was right—she didn't have to go so *hard* all the time. She was allowed to just be a twenty-year old college student once in a while. She could hang out with her boyfriend, sleep all day, play on his Wii, make love and just be ... silly and aimless and ... young. The way they had been during Winter Break. She would talk to him about his dreams, as much as she expected him to listen to her when she talked about hers. She would ...

Her phone chimed, and Zora looked down at it. Shad was outside.

Standing and grabbing her overnight bag, she took a deep breath. One would have thought the interview was tonight, going by how nervous she was right now.

"Breathe, Zora," she said as she opened the door. "*Breathe.*"

"Talking to yourself?"

Deuce was standing there. Her entire body sighed, and almost immediately her eyes filled, from gratitude. And with joy.

"What's the matter?" he held her chin between his thumb and forefinger, and kissed her quickly on the forehead. "You nervous?"

"No." She shook her head. "I mean, *yes*. But ... I'm just ... I'm happy to see you."

"Mia gave me your flight details," he explained.

"Where *were* you all day?" she asked. "You didn't call, or ..."

"I figured you were busy preparing and I needed to give you that space."

Zora shook her head emphatically. "No," she said. "No space. I don't need space. Not from you."

Deuce smiled and took her keys from her, locking the door. It was only then that Zora realized he had a bag too. A medium-sized duffle, slung over his shoulder.

"I heard what you said this morning," he said, handing her back her keys. "That sometimes you just need my presence. If that's still true, when you do this interview, I want to be present."

Zora got on her toes and wrapped her arms around his neck. "Yes, please."

"You think your ex-boyfriend will mind me ridin' with y'all to the airport?"

"I think he'll welcome it," Zora said. "Because he kind of knows ... whether he admits it or not."

"Knows what?" Deuce asked as they headed down the hall.

"How much I need you there."

"You do?" He looked at her.

"I do." She leaned into him and Deuce draped an arm over her shoulder, pulling her closer against his side.

"You know New York's my town, right?"

"I do know that, yes." Zora smiled, thinking how much calmer she felt already. Just having him near, and knowing he would be with her for one of the most important days of her life in social activism made her feel more centered.

"So, while we're there, we might as well have some fun." Deuce suggested. "Maybe stay through the weekend. You down for that?"

"Yeah," she said. "I'm down for that."

THE FLIGHT WAS A SHORT ONE, and by ten-thirty that evening, they were installed in their hotel, a few blocks from the CNN Columbus Circle studios where the interview would be filmed. Rashad, who hadn't registered too much of a visible reaction at Deuce joining them, went straight to his room, with plans to meet downstairs at four-thirty a.m. Zora suspected it bothered him somewhat that Deuce was there, but Shad was the consummate professional when it came to BLM. He wasn't one to allow something like his ex-girlfriend's new man to distract him from his path. CNN was potentially his launching pad, and there was no way something so trivial as a romantic rivalry would derail that.

Exhausted, more from the roller-coaster of emotions throughout the day than the lateness of the hour, Zora took a quick hot shower and then collapsed on the massive hotel bed. CNN had sprung for an almost palatial suite, and there was even a welcome basket awaiting them when they checked in. Deuce, who was completely accustomed to posh accommodations, had taken it all in stride, while Zora spent a few long minutes staring out at the stunning view, before her eyes became heavy.

She opened them again only when she felt Deuce climb into bed next to her after his own shower. He was warm, and smelled fresh and soapy. Zora positioned herself so her head was on his chest. The room was almost completely dark, except for the lights from the Manhattan skyline.

"I'm sorry I was so selfish," she said.

"Get some sleep," Deuce responded.

"I will, but I just wanted to say that out loud, first."

"Now you've said it, so go to sleep."

"And I always took for granted how much you wanted this

to work. I think I took it for granted from the very first time we were together, and ... I always let you put yourself out there first, and take all the risk, and I just ..."

"You sure like to make speeches," he said, amusement in his voice. "You'll do just fine tomorrow."

"Don't make a joke out of this," Zora said rolling over so she was on top of him. Cupping his face in her hands, she forced him to look at her. "I don't want it to always be you, taking the risk, putting yourself out there. So, I want to say it first. I'm ... I'm in love with you." At the stunned look on his face, Zora felt her heart rate double. "And it's fine if that's not how you feel yet. I don't care ... I mean, I *care*, but ..."

Deuce lifted his head and kissed her, effectively putting an end to her "speech."

"I love you, too, Zee," he said when he let his head fall back onto the pillow again. He shook his head. "You just don' know ..."

Zora smiled. Because once he said it, she realized that she already did.

She did know.

———

"YOUR STORY STRUCK a chord with me personally," the host said, smiling at Zora and Rashad. He was handsome and affable, with a perfect face for television, boyish, and of indeterminate age. "Because people are so accustomed to thinking of millennials as somewhat self-centered, to see your commitment to this difficult cause, and I understand, to each other as well ... it's been heartening, I think for a lot of people."

"Well, we *are* committed to each other," Rashad said, turning on his best and most telegenic smile. "That's true. But as friends. And as compatriots in a cause that we actually don't think is that difficult."

"Wait, so you're not ..."

"Dating? No," Zora jumped in. "But we understand why that's intriguing to people. Young, Black couples, young Black *people* are so seldom represented in that light, so the fascination is natural. But what we're focusing on is something very specific ... how the lack of positive images and attitudes about the Black community in general can lead to tragic consequences that I think no one would want to see."

"But isn't one of the rallying cries of your movement that some people *do* like to see it? That specifically law enforcement is overtly antagonistic toward the Black community?"

"Look, some people like to caricaturize BLM as saying that law enforcement is out there hunting Black folks; and yes, there *have* been some instances of explicit bias that can't be ignored." At that, Rashad paused to let the weight of the comment sink in. "But by and large, we argue that the *implicit* biases against Black people in our society are also present, and evident in law enforcement. Including in cases where deadly force was used. Many times, unjustifiably."

"So, talk to me about why you're not more focused on Black-on-Black violence," the host challenged. "If Black lives matter, shouldn't they matter even if the shooter isn't White?"

"Absolutely," Zora said. "But let's start with debunking the myth of Black-on-Black violence ..."

"How is it a myth when statistics show that Black people are more likely to be killed by a Black person than by someone who is White?"

"Because the statistics for Whites are comparable. Yet we don't call that White-on-White violence. We don't imply that there's something particularly pathological among Whites that make them cannibalize their communities. Violent crime, no matter how committed or by whom, is something we all care about," Rashad said, his tone becoming more impassioned. "But we're not a movement about generalized violent crime in America. There's plenty of folks working on that, and we wish them Godspeed and success. BLM is a movement focused on the illegal use of police power to deprive Black citizens of their lives, motivated by bias—whether implicit or explicit—under the color of law."

"Well that's as clear a statement as I've ever heard describing what you're fighting against ..."

"Not against," Zora said smiling. "*For*. What we're fighting *for* is equal justice under the law."

"Okay," the host said briskly, glancing surreptitiously toward the time-keeper. "So I guess we'll have to leave it at that. But I know people will want to know. No chance of a little romance between you two?"

"No," Zora said, looking at Rashad. They exchanged a smile, then her eyes drifted just off-camera to where Deuce was watching. He winked at her. "Where romance is concerned, I'm all good on that."

"HOLY ... it's the whole *building*, babe?"

"Yup. This is SE. The company my father built."

Zora leaned back and looked up in the enormous atrium, with glass ceilings that extended three stories high. And beyond that, were the working floors of Scaife Enterprises—twenty floors apparently, all teeming with people who worked for Deuce's father. It was different, seeing the source of the wealth than it was seeing the wealth itself. Lots of people had large and imposing homes, but few could claim to have built something like this.

Zora thought back to the reserved, man-of-few-words who had been introduced to her as Chris Scaife, and was suddenly even more impressed than she had been then. Her impression of him wasn't of someone who was modest or unassuming by any means, but now, being in his building, she couldn't understand why he wasn't downright arrogant.

"Jamal's waiting for us on the twentieth," Deuce said. They were waved in by the desk guards, and ushered to a private elevator which required a code once it opened. Deuce punched in five digits and then they were off.

Zora stood on one side of the elevator watching him as they ascended. He looked comfortable, but not cocky. Chris Scaife, Jr. wasn't arrogant either.

"What?" he asked, grinning when he caught her staring.

"I don't know. I just ... you should be a lot more of an asshole than you are, given all of this."

He laughed. "Thanks, baby."

"No. You know what I mean." She crossed the distance between them and leaned into him, letting her head fall back so she could look him in the eye. "It's just ... a lot, that's all."

"But it's not mine," Deuce said. "Not really. I didn't *make* any of it. Why would I be an asshole about it?"

"That wouldn't stop most people from puffing their chests out a little bit, Deuce. Believe me."

"Maybe. But for me? Just means I have that much more to prove."

Getting up on her toes, Zora kissed him, contemplating for the first time how little credit she had given him. For being the man—yes, the *man*—he was. Despite all this, rather than because of it.

Just then, the elevator came to a halt and the doors slid noiselessly open.

"*C'mon*, man," a booming voice said. "Don't be makin' out with your girlfriend on the company elevator."

Deuce turned and grinned, and Zora watched as he exchanged a half-hug, half-handshake with a ridiculously good-looking, well-built man with a complexion just a couple shades lighter than her own.

"Jamal, this is my girl, Zora," Deuce said. "Zora, this is Jamal Turner. He's President and CEO of Scaife Enterprises."

Jamal Turner smiled and looked her over as she stepped off the elevator and took his hand. "You *are* beautiful. I was at your school a couple weeks ago to talk business. And all he wanted to talk about was you. Now I can see why."

"Hi," she said, blushing. Jamal Turner was the kind of man who could, with one appreciative look, make a girl lose her power of speech.

"Okay, so Deuce said you need the grand tour. So let's do this," he said. "You ready?"

"Ready." Zora nodded, taking a deep breath.

She was just a *guest*, and felt intimidated by the scale of the place. One day, Deuce might have to assume control of all this. The idea he had, of a small artisanal label, cranking out "real-deal talent" seemed modest by comparison, but made sense to her now. He didn't just want to take all this over, he wanted to create something of his own. So maybe one day he would feel worthy of assuming control.

He'd told her once, and she didn't understand what he meant then, about the weight that came along with being "the exception." But she was beginning to understand a little more. This was all pretty darn weighty.

Her shoulders heaved once again, as she looked ahead at the opulence of the offices, the crisp attention to detail. Suddenly, she felt woefully underdressed in her jeans and casual long-sleeved tee.

"Hey." Deuce's voice snapped her out of her reverie. "You good?"

"Yeah," her voice was a croak.

"It's kind of overwhelming, right?" He sounded almost apologetic.

Zora nodded, looking up at him; and seeing him for the first time through her new perspective. He had never looked more amazing.

"*Keep up, love-birds!*" Jamal Turner was calling back to them from several paces ahead.

"Here," Deuce said, his eyes on hers, his voice strong and confident. "Take my hand."

Zora took it. And held on tight.

ALSO BY NIA FORRESTER

The 'Commitment' Novels

Commitment (The 'Commitment' Series Book 1)

Unsuitable Men (The 'Commitment' Series Book 2)

Maybe Never (A 'Commitment' Novella)

The Fall (A 'Commitment' Novel)

Four: Stories of Marriage (The 'Commitment' Series Finale)

The 'Afterwards' Novels

Afterwards (The Afterwards Series Book 1)

Afterburn (The Afterwards Series Book 2)

The Come Up (An Afterwards Novel)

The Takedown (An Afterwards Novel)

Young, Rich & Black (An Afterwards Novel)

Snowflake (An Afterwards Novel)

Rhyme & Reason (An Afterwards Novel)

Courtship (A Snowflake Novel)

The 'Mistress' Novels

Mistress (The 'Mistress' Trilogy Book 1)

Standalone Novels

Ivy's League

The Lover

Acceptable Losses

Paid Companion

The Makeover

ABOUT THE AUTHOR

Nia Forrester lives and writes in Philadelphia, Pennsylvania where, by day, she is an attorney working on public policy, and by night, she crafts woman-centered fiction that examines the complexities of life, love, and the human condition. Subscribe to Nia Forrester's Newsletter for free reads, exclusive samples, short stories, giveaways and more: https://bit.ly/2UorIXl

Reach her at: authorniaforrester@gmail.com